OUTCAST

Outcast

*Mountain Warriors
Book 1*

R.J. BURLE

Pier House Books

Copyright © 2020 by R.J. Burle

All rights reserved. No part of this book may be reproduced in any manner whatsoever without written permission except in the case of brief quotations embodied in critical articles and reviews.

First Printing, 2020

Thanks to God for blessing me with my wife and (harsh :)) editor, Amy Willoughby-Burle, who is also a published novelist that you should check out.

Forward

Foreword by Author Eric Hildebrande

I started writing what you are about to read less than a year ago. This story has already been told, documented in film and audio. Whether that has been shared, I may never know. I only wrote this log down in the case the film was destroyed. To be honest, at first my desire was for fame and fortune as a journalist and documentarian. Now, my motivation is simply to make sure that this is written in the history books. I may be dead when this gets out. This writing may be the blunt and final epitaph on my tombstone that never was.

On the surface, this should be a good read of survival, warrior arts, and practical living skills of a tribe surviving in the wasteland of the Forbidden Zone. However, after recently reading it over, I realize that I was a bit arrogant and not as mature ethically as I am now. Originally, I embarked to demonstrate how to survive in the woods in a post-apocalypse America. However, it was an education on learning to survive more inside myself. When facing the reality of death on a daily basis, what really matters in life becomes much clearer.

The true terror is not with vampires, zombies, or another diseased variant of human and non-human remains in the terror of the wilderness, but rather what lies deep within us all. This may sound cliché, but I find that bears repeating to all and most especially to myself.

| 1 |

I felt like exploding, but contrary to my feelings, I sat at the bar like an immobile lump. My life was going nowhere. I had just lost my job during the worst depression in history, literally of apocalyptic proportions. My girlfriend, or ex-girlfriend rather, was reported to be cheating on me with a friend of mine. Who that friend was, I had yet to identify through the rumor mill.

With my little realm crashing down, I tried to focus on the big picture. The world in general was majorly screwed and a breach of the quarantine wall from The Forbidden Zone would turn the major screw into a total screw.

I was a journalist. Big emphasis on "was." I should have been on the front lines covering this tragedy of catastrophic proportions, but I didn't know how, or even if, the new government would allow me to cover it. Martial law was the rule at the moment.

Even in the smaller picture, I seemed to be having a major breakdown inside of me that coincided with global events.

I was at that odd point in my life when you realize that all the dreams of hitting it big from your teens and twenties can evaporate into drudgery until death. I either had to do something, anything now, or just accept nothing for the rest of my life.

I was in a dive bar in Northern Virginia, just outside of Washington DC, but close enough to still have the big city vibe. The establishment was a dump as most places had become. Colorful, cheap plastic décor attempted to give a feeling of high life but failed abysmally. Especially since the cheap decorative material aged quicker than a bar hag's face. The Powers That Be guilted us into doing away with the disposable lifestyle for the sake of the environment, but instead of doing away with disposable products, they convinced us that low quality crap was reusable, indefinitely.

Speaking of crap, I was drinking what now passed as beer after it all went down. I drained the last warm remains of my fifth, sixth, hell, and maybe even seventh reusable plastic bottle of swill and ordered another. It was a good night when you couldn't even remember the amount of pollution that you subjected your body to. However, many it was, I needed another. The earlier drinks did nothing to ease what frustrations stirred deep inside of me. Where the brew lacked flavor, they over-compensated by adding distilled spirits therefore making a very potent beer.

I took a drink of my new beer. It was ice cold, so I could hardly taste it. Glaring at the TV, I actually startled myself as

I suddenly blurted to the world, "This is all just a bunch of crap!"

Although my inner longings weren't stifled by the beer, my powers of reason and restraint were definitely impacted to a high degree.

"Shut up, man!" Tommy ordered from the seat beside me. He raised an open hand at me like a traffic cop ordering a line of cars to halt, but his eyes stayed locked on the TV screen above the bar.

I tended to avoid watching anything put out by the mainstream media. My dislike was based on a combination of fear of being influenced by the garbage and possibly a bit of jealousy. A jealousy because all the glory they achieved should be my own. Anybody could pump out the crap that passed for entertainment. Why couldn't I? However, this show was Tommy's baby. In fact, the show had started with a pre-recorded segment of him introducing the new episode in a faux-professional voice. I thought it looked forced, but everyone else seemed to believe that he was genuinely concerned for those in the outlands. In fairness to Tommy, my cynicism may have been due to my over familiarity with him through the years.

Tommy was in the circle of friends that I had grown with, and I knew I would most likely continue to cling to this friendship because there seemed to be nothing else. However, Tommy was by far the most successful person that I knew other than my Uncle Daniel Hildebrande, the current Governor of this FEMA section, of course. He answered to no one.

I shot back at Tommy, "Dude, why should I shut up? The drones don't pick up any sounds." I protested the obvious, but the other patrons glared at me. I then mumbled weakly, "You can't hear anything, anyway."

The people surrounding me were all professionals. They wore gaudily colorful suits made of material that would have passed as extravagant burlap sacks in "the before." Everything these days was a show to pretend that life didn't suck.

At present, the patrons ignored me and went back to the mass hypnosis that the TV screen had induced. They were watching live drone footage taken from inside the Forbidden Zone. The national networks had just begun to experiment on a new angle of entertainment. To fund the defense of the quarantined Southeast FEMA Corridor and possibly a nefarious black budget of secret experimentations, they were using security drones to film the inhabitants in their daily lives and profiting from the entertainment value that was live streamed on national television. It could be something as mundane as watching a woman start a fire using a bow and drill to something as catastrophic as watching a zombie horde destroy an entire settlement. As the FEMA Director of Intelligence Gathering, this was Tommy's baby. He was on the cusp of a combination of media stardom, great wealth, and a higher position in government. The dreamed of trifecta.

I should have been happy for my friend. Instead, I looked up at the screen, angry that journalism seemed to be replaced by drones, much like the factory worker was once angered by the robots that replaced him in the auto plants, but who would be crazy enough to willingly go into the quarantined zone? That was strictly a one-way ticket, both figuratively and literally.

I put aside my anger as I looked to the TV. This episode of drone footage actually caught my attention. Really, it was the people themselves in the film who caught my attention. You couldn't help but feel the passion in the grim determination and hope on the faces of the refugees getting filmed. Four people trekked a trail in the high Southern Appalachian Mountains. They had a definite vibe of being a family. It was led by a man with ragged clothes, a huge pack on his back, longish hair and a short beard. Although exhausted, his eyes were ever vigilant. Two weary children followed him. Bringing up the rear was a worn-out looking woman carrying a baby. Despite her unkempt appearance, I could see that she was a very beautiful woman. Oddly, I found myself falling for her. Her eyes were so expressive. The journalist in me desired to know her story.

Everyone in the family except the baby had multiple weapons on them. I guessed there was probably a small knife concealed in the baby's wrappings as well for the mother to grab if needed.

The father had a battered M-16 looking gun that hung on his shoulder, probably something cobbled together during their two years in the post apocalypse world, a handgun at his hip and two swords strapped to his belt. The wife and children seemed to keep their weapons and valuables more concealed. Although from prior experiences in warzones, I could see the bulges of the concealed weapons in strategic places like the waist and under the shoulders. I had the feeling that the man wanted himself to be the target as added protection for his family.

As much as the lady with the deep eyes captured my attention, I still desired to stick to my guns as the cynic in the room. "Big deal," I said. "Some survivors are taking a hike."

"Quiet!"

"Shut up."

A few random voices scolded. I didn't bother to look at them as I sat with my arms folded across my chest.

I watched the screen as the father looked up and ahead, and stopped. He held up his hand, signaling his family to halt.

Tommy pointed up to the screen and spoke in a tone like he was mocking his own TV voice. "The dude senses something awry. He knows it's someone or something else. Robbers? Zombies?"

"Yeah. This is about to get good," someone behind me said. I could hear the speaker's feet stepping nearer to the TV to get a better view. Unfortunately, I could also smell his BO covered by even more offensive cheap cologne. I noticed that when people picked a bad cologne, they wore it heavier than someone with a decent type, and they were always the first to violate the social distancing ordinances of the quarantine.

"You deserve a Captain Obvious award," I said. I was tempted to say something about social distancing to avoid the spread of disease. I mean, I social distanced before it was cool, but these days it was seen as a geeky admonition.

"Quiet," someone hissed at me again.

I smiled at the annoyance that I caused.

A chill took hold of me. "Holy crap!" I exclaimed as I saw six cloaked and hooded figures in black in the far background on the television. They stood on the hill above as if waiting to observe the coming fight. "What the hell are those people?" No one else seemed aware of them, not even the vigilant father on the screen. "Are those the vampires that we've been hearing about?"

No one answered.

One of the vampires had a willowy figure, a woman. Despite the almost palpable aura of evil in the group, there was something attractive about her. I could almost see the depths of her dark eyes in the cavern formed by her hood. Despite the foreboding, there was something about her that grabbed me. Maybe as a vampire, she was the ultimate bad girl.

In my drunkenness, I literally slapped myself. With the issues with my current girlfriend, I found myself falling for anything with a skirt.

"Who are they?" I asked.

"Quiet!" someone yelled. I looked around but no one else seemed to notice the vampires or care.

On screen, the father directed his family to hide in a bushy stand of rhododendrons. In the winter landscape, it was the only tree with concealing foliage on the mountain. The father glared at the drone and flipped it (and us, the viewers) the finger. He dropped his large backpack and then boldly stepped forward on the trail as if he were alone.

He was instantly met by four men. The father pretended to be shocked by the chance encounter. The four men appeared to be genuinely surprised. Although we couldn't hear the words, it was obvious the four strangers were belligerent and by their motions were interested in the father's backpack.

The father kept talking, trying to calm the men. His hands were palms down, and he moved them in a relaxed manner as the four men circled and closed in. The father seemed reasonably calm despite the situation. However, I could tell that talking his way out was a losing battle. He seemed to realize this as an odd smirk spread across his face in acceptance of his fate.

As the men drew closer, he suddenly drew two katanas, thrusting his chest boldly forward with the action, holding both swords at his side. The points aimed at the sky as if challenging the very gods above him. His eyes glowed fiercely at the challenge. The smirk left his face as his grim lips formed a thin line.

The robbers instantly responded by drawing their own blades. One of the father's swords blocked a slash from one of the robbers. The other sword sliced through another robber's throat.

The three remaining would-be bandits backed up fearfully for a moment as their comrade fell to his knees, slowly choking on his own blood. Then they slowly advanced with their own weapons, swords and machetes, and returned the father's determined look.

"He's screwed," I said.

"I've seen him fight before. I think he stands a good chance," said Tommy.

"Yeah, he's good," the man with the BO and bad cologne agreed. He spoke right in my face, and I added bad breath to his list of offences, but I otherwise ignored him. The plight of the small family had my full attention now.

"Why doesn't he draw that gun at his hip?" I wondered aloud. Why didn't they all draw their firearms, I wondered to myself.

"Who cares?"

"Just watch!"

I was so drawn into the fight unfolding that I barely heard the few people who scolded me again.

The father was indeed quite the warrior. He didn't wait for the attack, but instead launched himself at the three men. His swords windmilled effortlessly. It was a continuous movement. One sword attacked as the other one retracted over his head to protect him like a roof from the rain of the robber's strikes and slashes, or his sword went to protect his side, and then the sword that protected swung forward to attack while the other withdrew back to protect. Every stab, slash and parry was so coordinated that his swords never banged into each other. His skill was beyond impressive.

Every Sunday, my hobby was to sword fight in the park with padded swords. I thought some of us were really good, but this guy would devastate us, all of us at once. He had less fear advancing into the razor-sharp cyclone than I had when advancing against people armed with something that resembled a pillow more than a lethal weapon.

The father actually seemed to be winning.

After about a minute, the father kicked out one of the bandit's knees. The robber dropped to the ground and didn't get back up. I was sure the leg was broken by the way he crawled to get away from the combat and from the pain registering on his face. His mouth opened in a silent scream and then closed in a twisted snarl. The other two bandits looked unsure for a moment but kept up the attack. It was so intense that even I would have scolded anyone in the bar who spoke up as I had done earlier.

Suddenly, the wife and the children broke from the hiding place. The mother held the baby in one arm and a machete in the other. The two children also had long knives in their hands. The two remaining bandits leered at the mother as the father scolded his family for breaking cover. Of course, I couldn't hear the exact words, but it was very obvious the gist of what was exchanged.

However, the woman and the children did not fight the bandits, but unexpectedly ran between the combatants.

"What the hell are they doing?" yelled one of the bar patrons.

Tommy grinned as he said, "Just watch." Despite the video being live, Tommy could read their reactions like a palm reader. I could only imagine the hours he spent in a darkened room as a voyeur of the Forbidden Zone.

The father and the two remaining bandits looked past the hiding place where the woman and children came. Terror registered on the faces of the combatants as they formed a circle facing outward with the children protected in the center. Suddenly, the former foes now seemed to be allies.

"Oh crap," someone in the bar muttered.

I swore as well as a horde of zombies approached the survivors. These weren't the typical shambling things from the old movies. These could actually shamble in a full sprint if they weren't too rotted. I watched the zombies pour around the six hooded vampires like a river flows around a boulder. I almost swore that the eyes of the beautiful female vamp saw through my soul through the drone camera, but that thought seemed insane. I recalled a news story of a schizophrenic patient who was charged with stalking a news reporter. He thought she was talking to him personally through his TV. I chalked my feelings up to drunken fantasy.

Some of the zombies immediately descended their slavering teeth on the men with the broken knee and the slit throat. I could almost hear the cries of pain from the men in the silent video feed. The close ups of the zombies terrified me. It wasn't their rotting flesh or anything else that was ghastly of course, but rather the inhuman hunger in their eyes. They were dead to any intelligent or cogent thoughts. Cats, dogs, cows, even snakes have more humanity in their eyes. With the zombies, there was just a fire for the desire to feed on live human flesh.

I was distantly aware of a chorus of reverential swearing from the bar around me.

On the screen, the husband, wife and two bandits put up an awesome fight, but they were so outnumbered.

"Come on, zombies! Get you some brains!" a patron in the back shouted through a laugh.

"That's messed up, man!" someone admonished.

The zombie fan retorted, "The sooner the zombies wipe out that scum and starve, the sooner the quarantined area will reopen."

There was some truth to that and the room quietly watched as another bandit was overwhelmed by zombies, dropped, and was devoured.

The two children cowered as the mother and baby, the father, and the remaining bandit tightened the circle and valiantly fought on as if they had always been a team. The remaining bandit was a very muscular man with a shaved head and a wickedly long thrice braided beard. He was actually a pretty good sword fighter. He would have been an even match for the long-haired father in one on one combat. He used both edges of his broadsword expertly. Where the father took out the zombie with one swing of each blade, the bald bandit sliced through two or three zombies with each mighty swing. I was surprised to see the bandit nudge a child to safety behind him as he continued to fight. The way the father and the bandit were now allies reminded me of how my cousins and I would fight each other viciously as kids, but we'd ban together as a team against any outsider who harassed us.

The mother used her machete one handedly and I hate to admit, but even with a baby in her hand, she would have easily whooped my butt and I had considered myself a pretty decent martial artist in the past.

Despite the skill of the fighters, it was a losing battle. The drone moved in for a close up of the father's face. In the middle of the fight, the man's glare seemed to pierce me. The raw determination struck me to my heart. I could read his lips as he yelled, "Duck," to the remaining survivors. That was the last I saw of him on that video clip; that determination despite standing before unavoidable death.

The father drew and aimed his handgun at the drone.

A chorus of angry curses erupted through the bar as the gunshot cut the video off.

The video instantly switched over to footage from another random drone. The camera showed a stupid looking person on the video. He stood, dully looking over a creek as he picked his nose.

The nose picker looked listlessly at the camera and flicked the booger. It landed and adhered to the lens showing a blurry footage. The drone moved erratically as if trying to figure out the sudden half blindness.

Everyone took their eyes off the screen. The real show was over.

"Why did he take time from a losing battle to shoot the drone?" I asked.

Tommy was furious and growled, "I would like to know that answer, too. They, especially that clown, keep ruining my drones. Especially whenever the footage starts getting good."

I was all questions. This really stirred up the journalist in me again. I felt like I was young and about to graduate from journalism school. I somehow, suddenly, found the same passion that I lost years ago. "And why didn't he shoot sooner? I mean, you don't bring a knife to a gunfight, right?"

No one answered. I really wanted to know why. The people around me had their visual meal. For me, it was just a cruel appetizer. It seemed that as a country, we had had one appetizer after another ever since this all went down, but no main course. The answers always seemed to be just around the corner, but each corner led to another wall with no answers. I could no longer rest, or I felt that I would truly spontaneously explode.

| 2 |

If you asked most people, they would say that the world ended two years ago when the dead began to walk. More correctly, when those who looked like they were dead began to walk, and not just walk, but eat those who still lived.

The governments of the world cordoned off great swaths of land to quarantine areas that were ruled by these zombie-like things. They curiously called the areas the "Forbidden Zones" as if they were trying to draw upon archaically hidden and dark fears that drew off of superstitious dread and religious taboos. In the before, I never would have guessed such hyperbolic language would be taken seriously in the modern age, but now, times really were that rank. Vast areas of agricultural importance, areas with minerals and oil fields, and areas that supplied what we thought were the necessities of life were off limits with the threat of instant death either from literal monsters, paranoid survivors, or government enforcers. Conspiracy theories served as news, propaganda as truth, and vice versa depending upon who you asked. No one trusted anyone, but everyone thought they had the truth. No one person who claimed to hold the truth agreed with another, and many people believed that that was done on purpose.

That was the game outside of the Forbidden Zone. Inside, the game was simply survival against every monstrosity imaginable from actual zombies to starvation. It was rumored that the population inside the quarantine area had been annihilated by 90% in the two years of the plague.

One the other hand, for many in the safe zone, the end of the world meant no longer getting cream in your coffee regularly. Most of the time it was coffee stretched out with roasted dandelion or chicory root. That was actually my only claim to fame. I did an undercover investigation into the one remaining coffee corporation. It was cutting ground coffee beans with dandelion root. I almost faced a lynch mob. People were so pissed at my reporting because it caused the cost of coffee to spike, by 85%. Did anyone wonder if that was because their coffee was 85% something else? No! They preferred coffee, no matter how diluted, at a price they could afford.

Even worse, I caught heat from my uncle and adopted father, the governor. With the same last name, the fire from both his constituents and the corporation that cut and sold the weakened coffee caused him to sink in the polls. To see all my work paid off in scorn still stung me.

We also dealt with regular rolling blackouts, leaving us without electricity for an hour or two-- that was the "tragedy" of modern life. It made me laugh out loud thinking about that as a tragedy in retrospect, but the government tried hardest not to ensure food, transportation, energy, and other essentials were in supply, but to ensure continuous streams of entertainment to forget that life was horrible.

Oddly, an entertainment shortage was the only thing to make the populace riot. While everyone's lifestyle went to hell, we were still entertained by two very different styles of shows. One was the countless reality shows of celebrities living it up like people did in the before. These were as vapid as ever, but I guess it gave people hope that a return to easier times was achievable, if we just kept faith in the authorities.

The other type of entertainment was the experimental drone footage of the FEMA quarantined zones. Tommy was attempting to combine his government connections with his natural showmanship to catapult himself as some Media Entertainment Governmental Complex celebrity. That may sound like a conflict of interest, but at that time, government officials not only had unlimited powers, but if they could keep the populace entertained and content enough not to riot, they had pretty much free reign to do anything. The populace, though on edge, was extremely forgiving if offered a treat.

***

As the bar went back to scattered conversation, Tommy turned to me and said, "It sucks they can't do something like a documentary in that area. You know, like *Survivor Man*. Where they film people, you know, surviving. It would make some more bucks than this venture."

He gestured to the drone footage on the TV screen. Now, someone on the screen was petting a feral looking dog. Both animal and man shared the same hangdog face of living right on the edge, but there was a friendship between the two. I was expecting the person to get bitten or something, but nothing dramatic happened. I mean, neither the dog nor man looked inclined to such violence, but to make it on TV something inside of me expected such drama and Tommy knew it.

"Why can't we do that?" I asked. It wasn't a rhetorical question. "Why can't someone go in and document the life? I mean, the drone footage is missing the human touch that only an interview could give."

Tommy looked at me as if I had been bitten by those zombie things and laughed. "Are you nuts? Who the heck is stupid enough to sneak into that hell hole? Anyone who tries to return from the Forbidden Zone would be shot on sight and incinerated, even if they did survive the horrors. Hell, you know that."

"That's what a good journalist does. That's what someone with a vision and balls will risk," I answered without considering what I was saying. I felt totally sober. The alcohol could not stem the flow of my thoughts, my goals and dreams.

"Again," Tommy snorted with cynical laughter, "Who the heck is that crazy?" He paused and asked skeptically, "You?"

He looked into my eyes as if reading my thoughts and laughed a full belly laugh. "Dude, you wouldn't last. You are a total wuss. You dropped out of journalism school before going back and finishing! Even when you tried to freelance it in the Middle East and South American war zones you flaked out and had to call your uncle to pull some strings to bail you out of there multiple times."

I remained silent as those old wounds were ripped open. I had been athletic, studious and ambitious. It was just in the last year, I succumbed to alcoholic decadence.

Tommy laughed again. This time it was more sober, like a snort when someone finally figures out an answer to a long-standing problem. It was an answer that sat right in front of your face like a stubborn drunk at a bar who refuses to leave at closing time.

"What?" I asked.

"Your eyes," he said looking into my soul.

"What about them?" I pressed.

Tommy held his thumb and forefinger in a rectangle and looked at me as if viewing me on a silver screen. He smiled quizzically at me and said like a TV producer, "You look both as determined and as crazy as that father when he shot out the drone."

***

As I stumbled out of the bar, I felt the alcohol weighing heavily on my body. In a way, when leaving a bar, I sometimes felt like I was beer itself being poured out of the building. Tonight, my legs had a hard time keeping up with the intoxicated energy of my mind as I poured into the street with the flowing crowd. However, the heaviness did not weigh down my thoughts. I felt like an eighteen-year-old again in my drunkenness. I felt alive. Drinking had made me feel that way for a few months as a teen, then it became a drudgery of numbness where I chased that energy to no avail. Suddenly, I wanted nothing to do with alcohol or anything else to numb me. I wanted to experience life to the fullest. I drunkenly vowed off alcohol forever.

I wanted to be somebody!

Tommy and I flowed with the mob of pedestrians heading out at the mandated closing time. The streets and sidewalks alike were packed with herds of partiers, ignoring the recommended social distancing. No one, except those with immense power, had operating cars these days. The only cars to be seen were abandoned and looted wrecks on the side of the road. Most buildings that towered over the people had shattered windows that would probably never be replaced.

Signs that warned of martial law had faded to the point of being barely legible. The list of rules was forgotten, other than not doing something stupid and standing out to the paramilitary police. You did not want them to notice you in any way. I shook my head as I saw some protesters who had odd qualities of both the hippie and punk cultures. They stood ahead of us carrying signs that said, "Free the Forbidden Zone!" and "The Outlanders are our kindred!" I understood, and in a way respected their love for others, but they needed to accept reality. As long as the virus ravaged the quarantined area, it would stay quarantined. I hated to sound callous, but that was the reality.

People were now heading home or to private (illegal) after hours clubs. Their feet crunching on shattered glass that littered all the sidewalks.

Occasionally people would come up and congratulate my friend Tommy. He was definitely a rising star, which only fueled my own desire to shoot through the sky.

"Dude! I can do it! I can!" I slurred loudly in Tommy's ear while we walked down the sidewalk. I stumbled and held onto his shoulder for support. I knew I looked like a typical idiot drunk, but I could not let this go. I feared waking up sober, forgetting this drive in me, and continuing to live simply and meaninglessly until I died.

Tommy stopped, righted me so that I stood straight and brushed his shoulder like my drunken stupidity might leave a stain on his nice suit.

He frowned, looked me over and simply said, "You are drunk."

That triggered something in me. He wasn't taking me seriously. As we walked to his government issued Lexus, I kept spilling out how much money I could make him as a journalist on the inside.

He kept brushing it off and rubbing my face in every past failure. It was infuriating me. It made my resolve all the more concrete.

I caught the glimmer of humor in his eyes and realized that he was intentionally provoking me. Tommy didn't just rise up in politics and entertainment without knowing how to evoke passion from people. Just what he was up to didn't dawn on me until later, but then it was too late.

Tommy stopped walking and grabbed both of my shoulders with his hands and looked me in the eyes. "Only someone with passion and resolve could pull something like this off," he challenged. "You have neither."

I returned his stance and grabbed both of his shoulders with my hands and glared right back at him. "Dude! That's the old me. I gotta do this. This is my last shot at something." Inside, I cringed as I could feel my head bobbing with unsteady intoxication.

I let go of him and cursed loudly at my drunkenness. I screamed my frustration to the night. I wanted to be taken seriously.

The late-night mob stopped moving around us and looked at us. I noticed two police officers in their black paramilitary fatigues glaring at me. Their grip tightened on their sleek, black assault rifles.

"He's fine, he's fine," Tommy called out. "He's just had a bit too much of a good time."

"The hell I am! I'm not drunk. You're not listening to me." I gave Tommy a rough shove.

Before I could yell or do anything stupid, the cops descended on me like attack dogs. Each one had a hold of both of my arms before I realized the trouble that I was in. I was going to get hauled away. We were in an extended period of martial law after all. They were supposed to keep the peace at all cost, and they were allowed to paradoxically use any brutality to enforce it.

I looked at their rifles dangling from their straps. I tried to remember some rifle disarms that I had half-assed learned in a martial arts class. Tommy could see the wild spark in my eyes. The look he gave me stifled any stupid attempt to escape.

Tommy stepped forward.

One of the police officers let go of me and pointed his rifle at Tommy and barked, "Step back, or you'll join him."

"Gentlemen, gentlemen," Tommy said calmly as he showed a badge that seemed to magically appear in his outstretched hand. I later found out that Tommy had rigged a contraption up his sleeve so his badge would slip into his hand when he activated a solenoid. Reaching for your ID too quickly could earn you a bullet from a spastic trigger finger protected by qualified immunity, and badges spoke much louder than words.

The police seemed hypnotized for a moment. The pointed assault rifles drooped as if suffering from erectile dysfunction. Tommy's badge was just short of gaudy for the high ranking. Had it not been for the fear it invoked, the overly ornate gold trim and a rainbow of colors actually may have been considered over the top.

They reluctantly let go of me, but I wasn't free yet.

One officer read the badge as the other one said, "Sir. We already tapped the emergency buttons on our trans-coms. We have to bring someone in when the reinforcements arrive. A false alarm can get us in trouble."

The officer reading it said, "Oh my God! This is Thomas Laurens the Director of..." The officer's lips quit moving. He looked at Tommy like he couldn't believe that he was actually there. Like he was seeing some avatar of a god instead.

"That's Senior Director Laurens," Tommy corrected with a friendly smile that didn't conceal his smugness.

The officer stammered slightly as he said, "Of course, sir. I love your work. I'm your biggest fan."

No one noticed me, so I rolled my eyes.

The second one swore and then blurted, "That's a cool device you have, sir, with the mechanism that puts the badge in your hand like that." The look in their eyes was a mix of fear and the kind of excitement you get when meeting a celebrity. I desired this respect even more as I watched.

"For safety purposes, I find the badge says more than words," Tommy said.

The second one nodded anxiously, "Yeah, we accidentally shot some guy last week--"

The first cop interrupted with a rumbling clearing of his throat and a glare at his partner. He then said, "Sir, the distress call for reinforcements..."

Tommy shrugged and held his palms upward as he reasonably explained, "I'm sure you men could find someone else causing trouble to warrant that call."

They nodded. We all wished each other a good evening. The police officers quickly stormed over to the protesters carrying the signs of love for those trapped in the Forbidden Zone. I looked away as I experienced a bout of guilt, not just because of what would happen to the protesters, but guilt that I was more relieved that it wasn't me this time. I heard the scuffle and protest. Then I heard a few cries with crashing blows and the protesters were silent as the crowd quickly looked away as if it never happened.

I was a little confused. Tommy usually let me get arrested and bailed me out the next day when I did something stupid. That way he'd have a good story to tell on our next occasion out on the town. This went back to our grade school days. I wasn't just a class clown; I was the lead class clown. If there was something crazy to be done that would bring the entire class to laughter, I was the one everybody, especially Tommy, dared. However, I let it go. Everybody changes, gets better with time, including Tommy. Me on the other hand, I seemed to get worse, but not tonight. I was devoted to making a change.

We walked past a block of buildings without a single window that wasn't busted out. I hated the sound of glass crunching under my worn-out shoes. In the past, shattered glass was quickly swept up. The glass under my shoes had probably been there for more than a year and would probably still be there until a strong enough storm washed it all down the sewer drain.

When we were far enough from the cops, I started up again, a little calmer.

"Hey, man. I'm serious," I said when we turned a corner on the street.

"I know you are, Eric, in this moment." He raised a hand before I could protest my sobriety. "If you're still serious when you can't crawl out of your hangover bed tomorrow, I will believe you." He shook his head as I still wanted to protest. He pointed a scolding finger in my face, "Uh uh. Tomorrow."

"Oh alright. Hey, let's hit The Underground." I said mentioning our favorite after hours joint. I pointed at my cell phone. I had checked the messages for the twentieth time since almost going to jail. "Jennifer still won't return my phone call tonight. I've heard rumors she's seeing someone on the side. When I confronted her, she neither confirmed nor denied it. She said it was just a friend."

He looked off in the distance and asked, "How did she neither confirm or deny, but claimed it was a friend of yours at the same time? What were her exact words?"

"I can't explain. You know women..."

"That can't be true, that she's seeing a friend of yours," Tommy consoled.

"Really?" I asked optimistically.

"Of course. You don't have any friends."

"Go to hell," I said laughing.

"It may be best. You wouldn't want to get arrested again?"

"What for," I asked, but already knowing his worn out answer.

"For dating out of your league. She is too good looking for you, man," he laughed.

"Yeah, yeah. So, what about the Underground?" I asked, not yet ready to go home. Not yet ready to face the fact that my girlfriend wasn't going to return my phone calls this evening or rather, this morning. I remembered my swearing off booze just a few minutes ago, and here I was wanting to go to another club. I was already drunk. I could follow through tomorrow when I was sober.

Tommy stopped walking, and I realized we had arrived at his car. I looked at the emblem of his office. It resembled the Presidential Seal except instead of a bald eagle there was a drone with four rotor blades. Without the emblem on the doors, thieves would have stolen, picked it apart, or at least vandalized the Lexus.

Tommy seemed to consider his response. He finally said, with eyes still in the distance, "I'd like to go to the Underground, but I can't. I—" he hesitated as he unlocked the car.

"Got a date with a good-looking woman?" I asked, nudging him with my elbow.

"You could say that," he said as he climbed into the driver's seat.

"Then you say it," I goaded.

"I have a late-night date with a very good-looking woman," Tommy said. He slammed the door in my face and drove away before I could ask for a lift to The Underground.

Instead of heading to the club, I turned, and headed home. It was for the best that I got a good night's sleep and avoided The Underground. My mind was still running at full speed. My dreams, goals, and ambitions were alive, almost screaming from the grave for vengeance against the years that I had neglected them. However, I realized, the first thing I had to do was go home, get a good night's sleep, and sober up. I actually jogged to get home faster.

I had never been afraid of the late night in the city before, but for some reason I felt that vampire woman had marked me from the TV screen. She watched me from every broken window of every blighted building. I rushed home along the darkened streets as if chased by the hound of insanity rather than actual hounds from hell. I desired nothing more than to wake into the daylight when the looming dark objects of the night made sense.

| 3 |

I woke up at dawn and was out of bed within moments of opening my eyes. In the past, I had never had a dream on a drunken night. I usually sleep like the dead until it is time to rise. That night however, I was plagued by the demons.

I was tempted to use a literary device to describe my dream so that the reader would have thought that I was describing a harsh reality, and then once drawn in, only then I would reveal to the reader that it was indeed a dream. However, I decided against that because this is supposed to be a documentary and I thought that would dishonestly yank at emotion, but also, I think it would take away from the actual horror that I felt in the experience.

At first, my dreams had flashed through the night as a collage of scenes from the drone footage. The mother carrying the child. The determination of the father. The terror on the faces of the children. The nobleness of the bandit to turn into a protector of the children. The slavering mouths of the undead. Their horribly fiery eyes. The belligerence of the robbers. The somber vampire figures who sullenly watched.

The dream then became very real. I walked through the dense woods with a sword in hand. I was in the Appalachian Mountains. The day was cold, misty, and dreary. The ground beneath my boots was spongy with water.

I experienced things like the weight of the sword as if they were real. Other things felt real although I had never felt them in the past. I felt confident that the refugee family led by the swordsman father actually survived. Yet I knew of no way they could have survived. I desired certainty to that dreamed knowledge.

The odd quality of this part of the dream was that the influence seemed to come from outside my head. In a typical dream, I might be a participant, but it felt like a movie, my movie projected on a screen in my head. Everything was from within me, whether conscious or subconscious. No matter how weird the story was, I knew that it was written by my subconscious no matter how deeply buried from my mind's awareness.

I know this all sounds odd, but in this sequence, I felt an outside presence imposing its thoughts, will, and very being into my dream and subsequently onto myself. It was not quite like a demon possessing the mind, but that is the closest I can describe it.

In the dream I stood in a darkened forest, in the high mountains, sunk deep into a cove. The sun had suddenly set. A drizzly rain misted. It was like I stood in the actual cloud. A ringed rock formation surrounded me almost like an amphitheater. The ground was marshy, but my feet floated above the water and the spongy mud beneath.

I then saw the female vampire. Armed with a slender and ornate sword, she walked in my general direction, but didn't look at me. I was an invisible and untouchable observer. She was also too enthralled with the forest around her to even suspect me. She was as at peace as a vampire could be. Her deep eyes looked over the woods with the fearless gaze of the ultimate apex predator. They were the eyes of a sleek feline, eyes designed to see in the dark.

Her beauty dazzled me. Her hood was folded back over the shoulders of her cloak. Her lustrous dark hair flowed over her shoulders. I watched her like I was a ghost who was confident of his ethereal presence. My excitement built as she neared. The feelings were simultaneously both fearful and sensual, and I was safe from her. She was no more aware of me watching her than she could have been aware that I saw her from the drone footage.

She walked closer, and I could have reached out and touched her were I in solid form. I could smell the sweetness of her pheromones. So faint, yet bold enough that I wished to bury my face in her hair and breathe deeply.

The forest slowly changed. I was back in my bedroom. She walked past my bed. I desired her, and I wished to take solid form.

She opened her red, kissable lips and seemed to talk to herself as she said, "This is no place for you…"

I felt terror strike me. I struggled to move, but I was suddenly held down by an unfathomable weight. I helplessly watched as she turned and looked straight into my eyes. She saw me and could kill me. Frozen, I couldn't move. Beneath the beauty I could see the evil spirit lurking in her eyes. I suspected it was the same spirit that caused this very dream.

"...Eric. You must not come here."

The weight was suddenly removed from me, and I shot bolt upright in my bed. I swore as I sat alone in my blankets. In the stillness, my breathing sounded like heavy equipment laboring. I instinctively looked around my studio apartment for the vampiress. I could have sworn she was there. With what had to be my imagination, I could faintly smell her, but I was alone with my terror.

I had only been asleep for an hour. It was a long way until sunrise.

I took a sleeping pill and a melatonin. I struggled back to sleep, but she kept taunting, smiling in my face, rousing me from my sleep. In the throes of the dreams, I couldn't pin my emotion for her: Fear? Arousal? It was like feeling all of my emotions at once. Despite her warnings and taunts, I could not let go of her pull. I had to see what was at the end of the metaphorical string that she had tied to me. Ironically, I felt a pang of guilt for spending energy on the vampire woman. Jennifer and I weren't officially broken up, yet.

Somehow, once awake and seeing daylight stream through the window, her image in my mind disappeared like a moon shadow in the harsh light of the summer's morning sun. With the morning sunlight, the passions for the vampiress were displaced by the curiosity of the plight of the family.

It was wishful thinking that dominated me. Despite the odds, I was sure that the father and mother had secured their family. They had too much fire in their eyes to die. If people with that spirit to live could succumb to death, who could survive? Their fight culminated in my own desire to fulfill my own destiny. If they could survive, I could too.

I stood from my bed and folded it up into a couch. The strewn sheets and blankets poked out. I didn't care. It matched the clothes, books and other objects that were scattered over the limited floor space. You'd think in a small studio apartment, I would try any trick in the book for more space, but the foldaway bed was the only effort I made. The studio was supposed to be temporary, but in the past few years it became home, and I resented it. In that time, I lived in that apartment like I would leave permanently any day.

I felt like I walked through a cobwebby fog to the kitchenette. I was still a bit drunk from the booze and woozy from the sleeping aids. The hangover was still a little way off, and I was hoping to beat it. I didn't have time for that crap today. Before sleeping the night before, I practically drowned myself in water in an attempt to rehydrate myself past the hangover. I probably drank over a half gallon and stopped just before the gag effect threatened to kick in.

I made some coffee with a stash of real bean, the full strength, that I saved for special occasions. This was legitimate coffee, uncut by roasted dandelions, other weeds, or chemicals. It was a valuable rarity. The special occasion I had originally had in mind was to impress a date. However, I needed the pure octane of caffeine today. It worked. Halfway through the first cup I felt like the sun's beams had pieced through an alcoholic dense fog. By the last drop, the fog was burned away. The path before me was clear.

I quickly got dressed to face whatever task was ahead. I then paced my studio apartment until it was seven o'clock. At that point, I was sure that Tommy was awake. He had remained relatively sober the night before. He derived more pleasure watching me make an ass of myself than indulging himself. Today however was a new day, and I was a new me. I would not drink again, ever.

I dialed his number and he answered the phone slow and tired, "Yeah?" His voice dragged that word as if it had three syllables.

I couldn't help but laugh. "Hey buddy! It's me!" I shouted with excess enthusiasm to mock his sleepiness.

"What the...? Eric?" Tommy mumbled. I heard him fumbling as if looking for the clock to see what time it was.

"Your phone has the time on it," I said.

"Yeah," he answered with irritation. "What the hell do you want?"

"Remember what we talked about last night? You said to call you first thing if I was still serious! Here I am! Wide awake and serious!" I said with a laugh.

"Damn you. I was sleeping. Hell, you should be comatose after the way you polluted your bloodstream last night," he laughed sleepily.

I heard a woman moan sleepily next to him. I couldn't hear the words, but from the fluctuations of the tone, it sounded like she hummed a question. I heard some fumbling as if he placed a hand over the receiver and scolded her.

"Um," he started to say to me.

"Is that Jennifer, next to you?" I asked jokingly, but it did sound like her.

He seemed to hesitate just long enough so I wasn't sure whether he actually hesitated or was just too sleepy to reply quickly and then answered, "Hell no."

"Just joking," I said, although a suspicion tickled an area of my brain that I couldn't scratch.

"Hold on," he said.

I could hear the creak of him sitting up in bed and the footsteps of him walking to another room. When he spoke again, he sounded sharp and fully awake. I could actually picture him in one of his Armani suits instead of pajamas, underwear or whatever he did or did not sleep in. Actually, I couldn't ever picture him without a nice suit. He probably had a tie and coat to go with his pajamas.

Tommy basically laid out the plan of my day. He instructed me where to go for a medical physical, for a passport to travel across the state, into Virginia, and a place to go for governmental secrets on the Forbidden Zone. My clearance would be in place by the time I arrived. The first place to go was a governmental office to get my own badge as a personal assistant of his. That title, as it were, would open some doors for me. I was amazed. It was like he had it all planned out for me. In retrospect, I feel like an idiot.

Before hanging up, I had to ask, "Hey Tommy? What's up with those vampire things?"

He paused about as long as he did when I asked about if that was Jennifer in his bed and then answered, "Don't even worry about them. They are one of the many doomsday cults of losers that occupy the Forbidden Zone. They're about as dangerous as the vampire wannabes that occupy the Goth clubs."

"Hey— "I started to say something else, but I heard the indistinct mumble of the woman calling for Tommy.

He said, "I'll talk to you later, bro," and he hung up the phone.

I pocketed my cell phone and immediately walked out the door.

***

I spent the day going from one place to another. At medical, I was surprised by how much blood they drew for tests. I jokingly asked if they would replace some of it. When the solemn doctor just looked at me, I then asked if he was a vampire. Despite my laugh, he did the impossible and frowned even deeper as he looked up at me from under his brows and over my chart. In fact, he seemed more obsessed with my file and only looked at me when I made what he perceived to be a poor joke. I was glad to move on until I realized that my next stop was the DMV.

The passport photo went much smoother. It saddened me that I now needed a passport to travel from Washington D.C. into Virginia, but these were the times that we lived in. It's the new normal. I heard that platitude a lot and it drove me nuts even though I caught myself using it. We'd resigned ourselves to tyranny.

When I arrived for my passport at the post office, they sent me to the DMV where they now took care of that process. Walking in the doors, I groaned when I saw the multiple long lines at many counters. The workers sat behind bullet proof glass. This was redundant since I had to walk through a metal detector where they took my very small pocket knife that was as dangerous as a toothpick.

However, once I stepped through the metal detector, an officious little bureaucrat ran up to me before I could get patted down by a goon in a uniform. The goon looked disappointed to be saved from the work. I instinctively looked for a name badge, but in martial law, they did away with name plates for government workers so they could maintain their private lives as they destroyed everyone else's privacy.

The bureaucrat kept looking between a photo of me and my face, and muttered, "Follow me, sir. We've been expecting you."

My connection with Tommy paid off.

However, I stood my ground. "Of course, but could I get my pocket knife back first? It's not even a weapon." I asked as I showed no inclination to follow him.

"Yes, yes, sir," the bureaucrat sputtered. "Of course. Officer Peterson, could you get his knife— er, I mean, pocket utensil and give it back? Thank you."

Officer Peterson scowled but followed the bureaucrat's request. I smirked at Peterson as I pocketed my property and followed the bureaucrat. I commented that I was surprised they didn't protect the convenience store workers better, they had a more dangerous job and a more crucial one at that, but the bureaucrat had the same sense of humor as the doctor, or more likely, I am not that funny when I am being an ass.

The rest of the day went smoothly until I received a text from Jennifer that said, "Call me immediately." I called her immediately and got her voicemail. I impatiently waited through the slow eastern meditative music that was too heavy on the sitar. Nothing against sitars, but when you were in a hurry to talk to someone and you heard the eastern version of elevator music, it grated on the nerves. After an excruciatingly long time that was most likely only a few seconds, Jennifer's recorded voice began. She had the sleepy voice of a faux-guru and I pictured her leaving the message sitting in a lotus position on a cloud with snowcapped Himalayan mountain tops behind her. The message said, "Greetings fellow journeyers. Let us stop the hate and be the peace we wish to be." The infernal peaceful music continued for another few seconds. After that pause, she continued, "Please, until we progress enough to channel our thoughts telegraphically, leave your mundane number." More idiotic music. I had never been so happy to hear an electronic beep. I left a message and she called me back an hour and a half later.

She asked me to meet her for coffee at four. It was a weird request, neither anything as extravagant as lunch or dinner. It sounded like she wanted a business-like communication rather than companionship.

We met fortuitously at the door to the establishment, each arriving at the exact same time. We greeted each other with a gratuitous hug. I tried to plant a peck on her lips, but she turned her head in disgust so that I kissed her cheek. This irked me. I am usually not too forward with affection, but if I had ever neglected to greet her with a small kiss on the lips, she would ask if something was wrong. She had insisted on this many times in the past. At this point, I felt like I knew the answer to my unasked question and buying a coffee and spending a few moments together was pointless, but we were here already.

Entering the door, I noticed that all the faux wood paneling and counters were very dark. I wondered if they had picked it because the color was similar to that of a roasted coffee bean or to hide coffee spills. We got a table and carried on some awkward chit chat until the barista brought our watered-down dandelion "coffees."

Jennifer had her head slightly bowed as she sipped her brew and looked up at me from under her brow and said, "You look alive." Before I could make a joke, she said, "Your eyes. They have a brightness that I haven't seen in a while."

I just nodded. I wanted to tell her about my plans, but spilling the beans on this plan could get me a bullet in my brain and immediate incineration.

After a moment of silence, she said, "Are you going to tell me what's going on?"

I smiled back at her and said, "I am kind of seeing someone."

She looked at me with a mix of scorn and perplexion.

"She's a vampire chick," I said with a mischievous laugh.

She glared at me for a moment and then laughed. "You always had the quirkiest sense of humor. That's one of the things I have always loved about you." She ceased laughing and asked, "Now what is going on?"

I replied without spite, but firmly, "That's the question that I should ask you. I have texted and called you, but you've been ignoring me. I also noticed you referred to my humor in past tense."

She leaned in and answered in a distant new-agey voice, "I have been going through changes in my outlook. I feel that I am on the edge of a breakthrough. I feel all the potential that I am capable of, yet I feel like you are an unchanging lead weight that is dragging me down. I need to either be free of you so that I can soar, or I need you to change so that you can soar with me. Do you understand?"

"I'm not sure," I replied. She was uncharacteristically blunt today, but the metaphors and platitudes still hid a lot.

"Of course, you don't," she replied in her mysterious faux guru voice.

"Listen, I understand your high-minded metaphors, but when you say breakthrough, are you talking about some new age platitude, are you talking about a career choice, romantic direction, what?"

"Maybe all of that and more, maybe none of that and less," she said, annoyingly cryptic.

I guessed that she was anticipating me being baffled. Instead I nodded like I understood and said deadpan, "That makes sense."

She looked at me with irritation. Then she said as if I had communicated my confusion. "I am a Zen Buddhist. We communicate in koans. They are— "

"--paradoxes, of course, or not," I said with a smile.

"Don't mock my path," she said.

"I am not mocking your path. When did you become a Zen Buddhist?" I asked with genuine curiosity.

"I didn't become one; I realized that I was one when I read an article last week in Vogue Magazine."

"So, the article made you realize that you are a walking paradoxical koan?"

"No, it's much more than that."

"Then what?"

She looked to the ceiling as if searching for a queue card. "It's so much more."

"And so much less," I said dryly.

She gave me a dirty look.

"How much more, then?" I prompted.

"It's like everything and like nothing," she said, struggling for more words.

"I got it," I said. This conversation was sucking more energy out of me than if she was a literal vampire at my throat. "Now, without paradoxical speaking, are we together, broken up, or in some limbo?"

At this point I realized it was most likely over between us. That was my logical mind speaking. However, my emotions told me that cutting those heartstrings would have me down in the dumps for quite some time. Despite getting on my nerves on occasions, I had grown accustomed to her quirks. Needless to say, I had my own definite quirks and she had accepted them better than anyone else in my past. I really didn't want to lose that. I felt like my sarcasm, which may have been self-destructive, was also defensive in preparation for the blow.

She straightened with determination, and I was thankful that she would be the one to break it off. I couldn't. However, she threw a wicked screwball. "I came here to break it off, but I see something new inside you. Your spirit seemed defeated in the past. Now I see a new fire in you. I still need a couple weeks to myself to get my mind in balance, but I'd like to stay together. However, you must tell me the change that has taken place inside you."

The barista walked by, and I ordered another coffee. I had a long story to tell, to get off my chest. Although Tommy was my friend, I didn't feel like he took me seriously. Everything was a joke to him. I vacillated on telling her too much. I faced immediate execution if she told the wrong person, but once my coffee was placed before me, the Hoover Dam couldn't hold back my words. It started as a vent as I recounted my shame of screwing things up in the past.

I then told her about the drone video and the people in it who inspired me. I told her about my desire to infiltrate the Forbidden Zone for a few weeks. I did make a point to leave out specifics that would leave a trail.

Oddly, she listened without interrupting with her usual tangents and platitudes. She looked me in the eyes the whole time. Her eyes widened so dramatically when I told her my plan for infiltration that I suspected for a moment that it was a poorly acted surprise and not genuine shock.

I finally finished my tale of new ambitions, and as I stopped, I realized that I was out of breath. After breathing in deep a few times, I took a sip of coffee and waited for her to react.

She nodded her head and almost blurted, "You are inspiring. I think that has great potential to make you a big hit and of course, bring out the plight of the outlanders. I love how you are thinking outside the box. It gives us a two-week break from each other while you do your job, and with Tommy's help--

I interrupted, "I don't remember mentioning Tommy. If I fail, I don't want him charged as an accessory."

"I thought you did mention him." She smiled and blinked her eyes ditzily. "If not, maybe I just assumed you needed him to pull strings to get to the access point."

"Yes, he is a powerful friend," I agreed. I looked at her. She could go from hard edged business woman to ditz and back in a second. It unsettled me. I suspected it as an act.

We chatted after that. It felt good to have discussed everything with a friend and intimate partner. I worried that my ambitions were insane, but seeing and hearing her encourage me placed my mind at ease. She reached over the table and took my hand. I held her hand and rubbed the back of it with my thumb. I felt newly in love with her. I felt like I could spend the rest of the day in the coffee bar with her and any trivial subject discussed would be stimulating.

After five minutes of small talk, I was about to suggest we grab dinner, but at that moment she quickly swallowed the last big gulps of her coffee and said, "I gotta go," and she abruptly stood.

We left the building, we hugged and when I tried to let go, she gave me that look. "Kiss me," she said.

We kissed on the lips. The passion spread from my heart to my lips and arms as I returned her embrace. She pushed away gently with eyes that promised something, not now, but definitely something in a few weeks. It melted my heart further.

We said our goodbyes and then went our separate ways. I looked back and saw she was on the phone. She gave me a worried look and quickly turned a corner. It placed a small lump of paranoia in the punch bowl of my passion for her.

Lost in thought, I stumbled into an old man who cursed me even after I apologized. I ignored him and walked on with my mind replaying what happened between Jennifer and me. In the course of our conversation, I resented Jennifer enough to break up at least three times and fell madly in love four more. I told myself that when I grew old, I should remember to have more patience with the tempestuous passions of the youth.

I touched my lips as I could still feel her lips and passion on them. As tight as our intimacy was in that moment, and the more I dwelt on it, it felt like a kiss goodbye.

| 4 |

A few days later, I walked into the belly of the beast. Just outside of Quantico, Virginia, Tommy worked in drone headquarters. The building was a gigantic former factory that once made some forgotten necessity. We sent those jobs overseas, and now our factories housed armies that spied on us. Based on the size of the buildings and the number of people employed, spying seemed to be our country's largest industry these days.

The ride there was uneventful other than the bus was thirty extra minutes later than the usual fifteen. I cringed as the lumbering vehicle approached, because with the delay, it had picked up far more people than normal. Its suspension was compressed so low that it looked like one of those low riders that were popular decades ago.

I crammed into the front accordion door, almost overwhelmed by the physical press and stench of the crowd. Somehow the human smell was even stronger than the diesel exhaust that spewed from the overworked engine. I squeezed past the people pressed together in the stairwell and paid the disinterested driver, dropping the money in the box. The bus was so full I couldn't get beyond the driver, or move back toward the stairs like the others apparently had. The people all around me moved en masse, like a wave from the bus's acceleration, and I was slammed and held against the windshield, pressed up against the driver, as the bus slowly pulled away. I was partially bent over the steering wheel and was blocking more of the driver's view. The engine barely picked up speed as it ground in protest beneath the weight of the mass of humanity and attained a speed barely ten miles an hour behind the flow of the light traffic.

"Look away from window and breathe!" the driver scolded me a few times before I could comprehend his thick accent. The smell of fermented garlic and cabbage seemed to amplify his angry tone.

"Why?" I asked.

"Can't see!" He flung an angry hand in the direction of the foggy windshield and wiped it with a greasy rag.

I unintentionally exhaled a pent-up breath and watched it fog the window he just wiped. I tried to brush the fog that I had just caused with my bare hand but it just smeared the water and grime. The driver irritably slapped my hand. He rolled his eyes and sighed heavily, and this time I could distinctly smell ginger with a touch of onion from his mixed fermented meal.

I looked out the driver's side window at the line of long dead cars that rested on long deflated tires and poorly stood guard over abandoned business with shattered glass windows. Transient people wandered in and out of the maze of damage. Miles upon miles of wreckage, both structural and human, and we were supposed to be the lucky ones, I mused. I actually looked forward to infiltrating the Forbidden Zone. It couldn't be much worse. In a moment of black anger at what society had become, I reasoned that at least the zombies would eat the human debris. I regretted the anger and hypocrisy immediately. Currently, I wasn't any better than a hobo myself.

The bus finally pulled in front of the leviathan where Tommy worked.

I pushed my way off the bus and entered the old factory building where I walked to the front desk in the cavernous lobby. After flashing my badge and ID to a porcine security guard who loved his minor position of power too much, I got a bit of the run around. I finally tired of it.

"Do you not recognize my last name?" I demanded.

He just looked at me as if I were the idiot.

"Look at the picture behind you," I said as I motioned at the smug visage on the portrait behind him.

The guard didn't move.

I explained, "The Governor, Daniel Hildebrande, the man with nearly absolute power, that's my uncle. Pretty much my adopted father."

The bastard still didn't move. He should have been scared, but I could see that he didn't believe me.

I was about to raise my voice, when his phone rang. He answered it, turned red and started sweating. I could tell that he was getting chewed out by someone. I could guess who that someone was. I gave the camera behind his desk the middle finger and started walking to Tommy's office.

The security clown yelled at my back, "Eric Hildebrande, Senior Director Thomas Laurens will see you now."

But I was already long past him. "Thanks, idiot," I muttered well out of his hearing range.

I walked through a rat maze of hallways and rode the elevator up to another maze complex. The hall cameras swiveled and witnessed my journey. An oddly robotic, yet sexy female voice from the speakers beneath the cameras told me which way to turn when needed. I obeyed.

I arrived at my destination. As I raised my fist to knock on a sturdy oak door, it swung open. I expected him to do that. Tommy has that persistent, mess with you sense of humor. He's not that funny, but he keeps himself entertained and that's what ultimately counts if you're Tommy. None-the-less, it still startled me. The situation, building, my ambitions, my new sobriety, everything seemed to be weighing on my nerves.

"Come in, brother," Tommy ordered.

I complied.

I walked past his attractive secretary, while Tommy glanced over me. I was dressed in the gaudy material that was by default fashionable due to it being the only choice. Tommy was dressed in a pre-apocalypse Armani that looked tailored and brand new. "Dang!" He said, "You look like one of those refugees from the Forbidden Zone already. I should call security for that beard alone," he said with his usual laugh. "Come into my office, we need to talk, but that beard... Dude."

I ran my fingers through my weeklong unkempt facial hair as we entered his office and he closed the door. The air in the room compressed as it sealed shut. My beard was a healthy five o'clock shadow when we last saw each other in the bar. It was borderline acceptable to have a well maintained five o'clock shadow. It was to be properly groomed to give the image that you didn't care, but mostly the current fashion was to be clean shaven to give an air of superiority over those bearded ruffians in the Forbidden Zone. I had blasted past having any of the fashionable grooming standards.

Tommy walked to his desk and fidgeted with something. When he stepped away, I noticed a framed photograph was turned upside down on his desk. However, his desk was cluttered with so much paperwork, that it may have already been faced down. It struck me as odd that despite his usual impeccable demeanor, his work space was a complete mess.

A large map of the world spread across a side wall like a quilt. It was mottled with striped zones that I figured marked the Forbidden Zones throughout the world. More than three quarters of the landmass was off limits as well as large swaths of the Pacific Ocean with many islands, whole countries in Europe and Africa, as well as the whole island continents of Australia and Antarctica. I swore as I muttered, "All of Antarctica is off limits? How did that happen?"

Tommy ignored my words and said, "The beard." He released a comically overdone sigh.

I wasn't sure if my lack of shaving was due to laziness combined with an overriding sole focus on my self-imposed mission or if at an atavistic level, I wanted to be like the swordsman I had witnessed. I had barely slept a total of a few hours in the days that passed since seeing the action on the barroom TV screen. In that time, I had gathered all my resources, worked overtime washing dishes at a friend's restaurant, and borrowed heavily from more successful family and acquaintances to acquire the latest survival, camping, and recording equipment. Any free time that I had left was spent looking over info about the Forbidden Zone. I was so ensconced in the study of that place that I was mentally on edge, like I was surviving there already. Most of what I studied was bootlegged topographical maps for backpackers before it all went down and other hard to come by info. The current government definitely did not want people to feel comfortable enough to attempt an infiltration into the Forbidden Zone.

Another reason for throwing myself with an abandon into this quest was that I really wanted to succeed. I wanted to impress upon Jennifer how badly I wanted to change our situation. She needed some space for a few weeks to sort things out, and that would be when I came out of the Forbidden Zone. She had accused me of being directionless, career wise, and she was right. I had lazily become a loser, no direction, no real prospects, and unemployed, but I was sure that if I could get some really good video, interviews, and stories from the Forbidden Zone and publish them anonymously through some of the channels that Tommy had connections with, I could be a rich man, in just a couple weeks. Everything in my life was riding on this venture.

After getting over the self-consciousness with the beard, I looked around his office. Just about everything except the hard, mahogany desk top seemed to be covered in a plush maroon colored leather. It fit his personality. Another hint at his success was that his desk was covered with paperwork. With great swaths of forest land cordoned off, limiting access to wood that made paper, most "paperwork" was strictly done on a computer. But top-secret information tended to be kept on paper because any computer could be hacked.

Tommy sobered and said, "You really are serious about this."

I didn't acknowledge with either nod or word, but he smiled as he saw the determination in my eyes as I simply stared back at him.

Tommy continued, "By the way. I don't think you're that crazy anymore. I think the potential profits far exceed the risks."

"Of course, they're worth the risk to you because I'll be the one in danger," I said with a wry smile.

He raised his hands, "Hey listen— "he started to say.

"Relax brother," I said. "I'm joking around. I would do this whether you helped or not. I need to chart my own destiny. I thank you for your help. By the way, what are those vampire things I've seen on videos?" I had already asked, but I wanted to see if his story changed.

He shrugged them off, "Who knows? Wannabes. Members of a doomsday cult? Maybe a mutant variation of the zombie virus changed them into that, or their immune system reacts to the virus differently. There is a bunch of weird stuff going on. That's why it's quarantined and why you should stay away," he ended with a laugh.

I started to laugh when I noticed a medical file on his desk among the books, charts, and files. The medical chart had my name on it and a check out date from two weeks before we even discussed me going in. I pointed that out and asked about it.

He hesitated and said, "They must have accidentally placed the wrong date on it. I never even reviewed your records until two days ago."

I picked it up and looked through it. He rounded the desk in a hurry and tried to take it from me. I held him off and saw something about a blood test that had been drawn after the zombie outbreak quarantined the Southeast, two years ago. They wrote something about the Hildebrande bloodline and DNA. I couldn't understand all the jargon from just a quick glance, but it said something about how it related to potential immunity from the zombie pathogen and something about vampires.

"That's top secret!" said Tommy.

"It's about my blood, so it is actually mine." I protested and placed the folder in my backpack for later reading. I then stared at him letting him know that I was keeping it.

"Fine, read it later. I don't care," he said. "By the way, would you like a drink?"

I zipped up my backpack and said, "Thanks, but no. I haven't touched anything since that last outing we had."

"I've got Jameson's Irish whisky," he said with a tempting smile as he rocked two drinking glasses side to side after he placed the bottle on the table.

My eyes widened. That was my drink of choice, and I had not been able to get it in the last two years, but I said, "No, I can't."

He cajoled me, but I stood firm. I gave one more refusal and he cracked open the fresh bottle and poured two drinks. "You can't leave me to drink alone."

That was my undoing, and as usual one drink led to another. He knew me like Jimmy Hendrix knew his guitar.

"Let's get back to our plans." Tommy said with a toast, "The hardest thing was acquisitioning the thousands of dollars for gasoline for the trip to North Carolina, but I can get work to pay for it, thanks to your Uncle."

I whistled. Gas was no longer at gas stations but at heavily guarded depots. I knew that fuel was scarce but I had no idea it was that expensive.

"You get more benefits from my uncle than I do," I complained, "but that's cool about the gas," I said as I toasted him.

I then looked out his window and studied the miles of blight that had once been a beautiful city. The whisky was hitting my head and my mind wandered from his words. Alcohol was definitely my undoing. I dwelled on how bad the times were these days. It was hard to believe that not long ago, a trip that far was nothing, maybe thirty dollars in gas.

"Check this out." Tommy held up a baseball cap as well as a vest and a waist belt. It had pockets for camera equipment, notepads and other stuff a journalist would need. In short, it looked like something a journalist would have worn in the jungles of the Vietnam era, now it looked like something an amateur would wear to try to look like a journalist.

I was sure that there was more to it than what I saw so I said, "It looks like something a dork would wear."

I was expecting Tommy to say something smartassed. Instead, he tapped his finger to four different points: the bill of the ball cap, both shoulders and the belt. "You can't see them, but those are cameras."

"Like a body cam?" I asked.

"Better," he explained. "They hook up to a computer and match the footage so that it looks like one coherent image no matter which lens takes the picture. The computer's program generates fill-ins in the gaps due to arm movement and other obstructions. It also makes up for erratic movement so the viewers don't get motion sickness. Its image is both sharp and reliable as long as at least one camera is exposed. It's waterproof and has solar panels for recharging as well."

All I could do was mutter, "Cool."

"It also comes with this," he said as he held a closed fist up near my face. His fingers sprang apart like a flower blossoming at fast speed. A little insect-like object flew from his palm. It buzzed around me with no more noise than a mosquito and then zoomed to a pocket in the camera vest when Tommy commanded it, "Go home."

"What was that?" I asked.

Tommy smiled proudly and explained, "A mini drone. It fills in the missing gaps from the other cameras. It also flies back to that pocket when its battery is almost used up and it charges itself in the pocket."

"Whoa," I said, genuinely impressed. "That's perfect. How much did it cost you?"

"Nothing, I snagged it from work. They're going to start issuing this to perimeter guards that work under us, but not for another year. After we make our fortune from the show that you film!"

"Speaking of border guards--"I said worriedly.

Reading my mind, he interrupted and said, "I will have no problem redirecting the drones. You'll have an easy, undetected way in and out."

"Cool."

He smiled and rubbed his hands together as he said, "But here's the best news. We have to leave tomorrow."

"What! Why?" I was a bit shocked and worried. As much as I had studied the situation and longed for it, up until now, it had all been in theory. I could always back out, but this needed an immediate response. "Why so soon?" I asked.

Tommy explained matter of factly, "I told them that I wanted to inspect along the outside of the fence, and that it was important to see the terrain and walk it to get a feel of how the drones fly. I'm expected there tomorrow afternoon. Even I have to follow official timelines."

I felt an almost literal weight on my shoulders. Every single hole in the fabric of my plans suddenly stood clear in my face like a mental confrontation. I needed more planning. "I can't go now," I blurted.

He smirked as he said, "I knew this was all talk. You never follow through anything."

He knew which buttons to push.

"Get bent!" I growled.

"That's the spirit," he said. "Let's have one more shot of whisky to celebrate."

I stared at the glasses and thought for a quick moment. Tommy was right. The sooner the better. "Sure. Let's have a drink to this endeavor, my friend!"

He nodded as he poured the drinks.

| 5 |

"A glorious day!" Tommy declared in a voice as bright as the morning sun. It was a rare, warm winter day and the sun rays smashed through the windshield and burned my eyes when I dared to open them.

Indeed, it was a glorious sunny morning that needled my brain through my dark sunglasses as we drove through the Shenandoah Valley. I should have enjoyed the beauty of the scenery of the seemingly never-ending ridge lines and the luxury of my first car ride in years, but I was horribly hung over.

Tommy had pressured me to drink shot after shot of faux tequila after we left his office. Meanwhile, he laughed off any of my suggestions for him to drink. This was typical of a night out with Tommy, but last night was an extreme. It was my send off, like breaking a champagne bottle against a ship's hull on its virgin float. Only in my case, I felt like the bottle had been shattered against my skull.

During that time, I lost track of my backpack with my medical file. Tommy insisted it was in his Lexus and I forgot about it until now. I let it go. I had more pressing worries.

We had left Washington DC at four in the morning while I was still drunk, and we would arrive at the border of the Forbidden Zone early in the afternoon or late in the morning. Tommy drove a pre-disaster black Cadillac Escalade SUV that was waxed to look shiny, black, and new like Darth Vader's helmet. I slouched in the passenger seat. Usually Tommy would have a chauffeur, but he waved that off for the sake of added secrecy. He laid the BS on heavy about wanting to save the taxpayers some money by driving the luxury SUV himself. The funny thing was that the Cadillac would burn through enough money in gas to hire a dozen chauffeurs.

The thought of the cost of gas made me shiver slightly. The punishment for sneaking out of the Forbidden Zone was an immediate bullet to the head and on the spot incineration. All the border patrol vehicles had a five-gallon tank of gas to promptly turn a violator into ashes. The government seemed to think it necessary to spend the money to burn away the memory of a potentially infected intruder.

A large emblem of Tommy's office was displayed proudly on the hood, side doors, and a final one on the rear door. This emblem was different from the one on his Lexus and was not for the entertainment branch but rather the intelligence gathering. The emblem on the SUV had an eagle with a telescope crossed with a rifle on its chest. I worried that it would gather attention. Tommy said it would do the opposite. That people near the border tended to look away from government vehicles for "safety" reasons. He told me that the enforcement arm had a lot more "leeway" with distributing justice in the border area, to put it mildly.

That may have been true, but something deep inside felt uneasy with the whole setup. Tommy was too relaxed, but then again, it was my life that was on the line, not his.

The closer we drew near the Forbidden Zone, the more his prediction proved correct. I saw a young mother, whose face was worn out before its time, not just look away, but push her children's heads away from our direction as well. It was surreal. I couldn't help but feel above it all, sitting high in the SUV, until I realized that it wasn't my power. I was simply leaching off of Tommy and that would be yanked out from under me shortly. With that realization, my headache thundered back.

Tommy laughed and pointed at the subdued people we passed. "See. Nothing to worry about. Your concern is simply from your hangover. I warned you about not over-consuming last night."

I shot him a dirty look which made him laugh. I didn't bother to say that he didn't warn me but encouraged me. He continued to laugh until I faked a dry heave.

"Hey! Not on the carpet. I don't want to drive back alone with nothing but the nasty smell of your vomit in the car as my last memory of you."

I stared out the window and smirked slightly with the knowledge that I actually got under his skin for once. I wish that I could have vomited just to mess with him. However, it wasn't until later when I replayed in my head what he had just said that I realized that I should have seen what was coming.

| 6 |

I was surprised at the great leeway and respect that Tommy's rank had earned him. The fierce, somber border guards followed his orders with as much zeal as they would bash in a lawbreaker's head. The chills it brought felt like ice water had been poured down the inside of my spinal column as I pondered the power that he wielded. For years I still saw him as grade school Tommy the class clown, or rather the instigator who dared me to be the class clown.

He stopped at a headquarters building near the border. Immediately after stopping, a big burley, bullet headed border guard sprinted straight at our SUV. I had never seen a man so tall and so wide who moved so quickly and fluidly. There was no sign of fat on his solid body. With the determination on his face and the speed of his sprint directed at our vehicle, I thought he was going to kill us. He had a black military submachine gun on his back and a handgun holstered on his hip.

I cringed as he opened my front passenger side door and said to Tommy, "Good morning, sir."

"Drop the formality, Don. He's cool," said Tommy, then he said to me, "Eric, Don will be something like your guardian angel."

"You got it, Tom." Don looked at me and ignored my outstretched hand. "Sit in the back, 'cool'."

I just looked at him blankly for a moment. Don's brow seemed to darken like a storm cloud rising. He was not used to being ignored. Before he could explode in a verbal torrent, I said, "Oh, no problem, sir," and I got out of the front seat and moved to the back. Don scared the hell out of me. I secretly wondered if he was brought along in case I got cold feet.

We drove off with Don and Tommy talking like old buddies. They also talked as if I was not there. I kept quiet. My hangover was starting to go away, but I was a bit unnerved with the realization of just how powerful Tommy was, and Don frankly frightened me more than a horde of zombies. I had never met someone who I was sure had killed another man, but somehow, I just knew that Don was a killer. He had a presence that was calm and cold on the exterior, but I felt like there was a neutron bomb about to detonate just under his skin. The fire in his eyes sank deeply in his impassive face, which made a bigger impression on me than anything that he said or how he said it.

One snippet of Tommy's and Don's conversation that I remember, and that I should have taken note of, was when Don said, "Hey, did you hear they may restart the old National

Football League. I really think if things had been different, I could have made pro."

Tommy nodded and said, "You definitely have the talent. However, what we have planned will be much bigger. Much, much bigger."

"You got that right," Don agreed in a deep growling voice that sounded relatively friendly.

We cruised along some meandering back roads as gravelly as Don's grunts, affirmations, and expletives, until we arrived at a path with just enough room for one vehicle to traverse. It had freshly laid, crushed white rock that paralleled the fence of the border. The fence and the road did not seek out convenience in the steep lay of the mountainous land, but rather followed a barrier drawn by a bureaucrat. I was no engineer, but I could see many instances where it would have been easier to lay both the fence and the road along a shallower grade. I could tell that the road suffered heavily from erosion, and regular new graveling was needed.

I stared with awe at the barrier. I had never contemplated just how high a twenty-foot-high fence was. It had multiple rolls of razor wire that were laced together and covered from top to bottom on each side. Warning signs of high voltage, infectious monsters, and immediate executions and incinerations from border guards were posted evenly and at a distance so that you could always see the warning.

We bumped along the winding gravel road for a while, and I lost track of time. My nausea from the hangover was gone, but the sick feeling in my belly was replaced with butterflies. We passed a small crowd of six zombies lingering on the other side of the border fence. I felt a chill as I realized what they were. From a distance, I had thought they were regular people, but their grey, decaying flesh gave it away. They looked out between the fence links with dull eyes, like a goldfish stares out of a fishbowl. For a moment, it was a letdown. I was expecting something fierce, deadly.

Then the movement of our vehicle caught their attention, and I could see their mouths opened in savage screams. Their eyes seemed to glow with a supernatural fury. They then launched themselves at the electrified barbed wire, and with a shock, three hit first and dropped to the ground. Although they had been electrocuted in front of the remaining three, the others still rushed forward and suffered the same fate.

"Are they dead?" I asked.

"No," Don answered. "Those dumbasses will get back up shortly. I think they actually get high off of the electric juice." He turned around and looked me square in the face and warned, "Don't you try to get a rush off the electricity. That will kill you in less than a heartbeat." He added a snap of his fingers for emphasis.

I nodded at the unnecessary admonition and looked out the window. We drove in silence. I disliked the way he talked down to me.

"Stop the truck," Don ordered his boss.

Tommy stomped on the brakes almost giving me whiplash as we skidded on the gravel.

Don opened the door and leapt out before the SUV came to a complete stop and announced, "We're here. Get out," he snapped at me like a drill instructor orders a raw recruit.

Tommy popped the back hatch for the trunk of the SUV from his seat. With no effort, Don pulled out a backpack that seemed like it was as big and as heavy as me. He tossed it right into my chest and I caught it. A smirk flashed and instantly disappeared on Don's face as the weight almost pushed me to the ground.

"Quit fooling around and put the pack on!" he commanded.

Under the heavy load, I followed Don towards the fence line. He bulldozed through a thicket of blackberry thorns like it wasn't there. I watched the thorns stick to his black and grey camouflage uniform. I didn't know if he was too mean to feel anything, if he didn't care, or if it was some tough guy act. I followed, but stopped at the briars.

"Hurry up," Don ordered.

I looked to Tommy who just nodded from the SUV, too intimidated to get out of the vehicle this close to the border. I was expecting my friend to see me off, but I didn't even get a handshake. Don obviously ran the show from that point on.

I swore and followed, cursing as the stickers bit me.

"Quiet," Don yelled louder than my cursing. "Your big mouth will give away our position."

I quit cursing the briars aloud and instead, cursed Don in my head.

I plunged through, with my eyes mostly closed and felt Don grab me by the throat and shake me. "Stop, you idiot," he hissed as he pointed to the sign that warned of getting shot and that there were 10,000 volts racing through the fence inches from us.

He led the way, still holding on to my lapel. We were now behind a rock formation where a boulder the size of a large car balanced precariously on a smaller stone. Don let go of me and kicked away some sticks and leaves on the ground to expose a small opening under the fence.

"Here's a steel pipe. It's wide enough to go through. Make sure you cover it back up when you emerge on the other side, OK? I will be watching from here," Don instructed.

Don't worry, sir," I said.

He grabbed me by the throat and pointed in my face. Despite the violence, he spoke in a very calm voice that was even more menacing. "Don't tell me not to worry. When you tell me not to worry, it tells me that you aren't concerned and that means you'll mess this up."

"Ok, I'll worry," I said in all seriousness. I didn't want to piss him off. I couldn't think because it seemed like everything I said and did in his presence was wrong.

He cuffed me across the head. "I don't want you to worry about it. Worry will cause you to screw up. I want you to focus. Got it? Focus!" he said as he smacked the top of my head like my grandfather used to smack his ancient TV when the reception was off.

"OK, OK." I paused then quickly added, "Sir."

"I will be back in two weeks for you. Don't come back late or early. Do you understand?"

"Yes, sir." I wasn't used to addressing someone as sir, but I did not want to piss off Don.

"Then get moving," he commanded as he pointed at the pipe.

I bent down and crawled into the hole. It was a tight squeeze, but I came to a complete stop with just my head in there. I was stuck because of the large pack on my back. As I backed up to take off my heavy backpack, Don yelled at me.

"You can't fit in there with your pack on, idiot."

I backed up and pulled the pack off and he tied a rope to it.

He instructed, "Drag it through when you get to the other side."

I nodded and plunged inside. Spider webs greeted me across the face. I spat and backed up as Don's boot kicked me hard in the butt. The pain of the bruise would last a week, but in that time, I would acquire far worse injuries.

"Move," he ordered.

I continued on through the horrid length of the pipe. I hated spiders and spider webs with a passion, but I hated Don even more.

It was a long crawl, maybe thirty meters, but with no light at the end of the tunnel, I suffered claustrophobia. I pushed aside a stone and some brush that concealed the opposite end and thanked God for the sunlight that streamed into my eyes. Pushing my way through, I finally scrambled out of the steel cave and pulled my pack through by the rope. I covered the hole under Don's watchful eyes from the other side of the fence. When I was done, I loaded my pack on my back. Although I looked the other way, I could feel his eyes upon me.

I looked and could see the SUV through the leafless winter trees, but not the driver's seat with my friend, Tommy. He wouldn't even get out to wave goodbye to me, I thought miserably. This hurt, but I realized that my hands were shaking. The weight of the job ahead finally hit me. I had to find and befriend the survivors who were most likely suspicious of outsiders. I must also avoid zombies, wild animals, and bandits. I was also feeling a second wind of my hangover returning as I brushed the nasty spider webs off of my face and clothes. I fought against a dry heave.

"Did you cover the hole well enough, like I told you?" Don asked in a growling voice.

Without thinking, I gave Don the middle finger. He kept glaring at me with the same level of malevolence as before. After looking at his unblinking features for a few seconds, I lost the stare down. I knew that I would face hell in two weeks when I came back. However, two weeks felt like an eternity. I turned to the mountains ahead.

| 7 |

I was soon swallowed by the woods. I could barely hear the SUV drive away as the thick stand of forest acted as a muffler. Even without leaves on the trees, the barren winter branches seemed to devour me. I was totally alone. It was an odd feeling. I was a city boy. I had only felt solitude in my own rooms, locked away in my privacy with constant forms of electronic entertainment controlled by my fingertips.

Although I was alone in the woods, I felt no privacy. I felt eyes upon me. Were they the eyes of people, bears, zombies, or my imagination? I didn't know, but I couldn't pull the blinds, draw the curtains, or close the door on the unseen eyes around me in the forest like I could at home.

The electronic noises I was used to were replaced by the chirps of birds or other things that I could not identify at that time. The high-pitched sounds of the unknown animals seemed to drill in my head over the sounds of my panting and the crunching of leaves beneath my feet. Even more unnerving was the scuffling sound of the paws and feet of the unseen forest denizens.

I purposely crashed through the brush to drown out the chirping of the animals until I heard a loud thrashing in the forest just to my right. It was so loud that my imagination pictured a zombie who had to have been a beefy linebacker for a top ten college football team before he was turned into his monstrous state. This linebacker zombie sounded like he was charging straight at me. The noise couldn't have been more than five or ten meters away. I couldn't see it, because whoever or whatever it was, was in a stand of bushes that still had leaves in the winter. I learned later that bush was a rhododendron tree; a miniature magnolia is the best way that I can describe it.

I stopped as I drew a multi tool. I fumbled with it to open the blade and dropped it in the leaves. I stood still, fearing to move, fearing to breathe, as I listened for more noise from my mysterious opponent, but all I could hear was my thundering heart that increased in volume, intensity, and beats per minute as I held my breath and held my feet still to avoid crunching the leaves.

Nothing. The lack of a follow-up noise unnerved me even more. How could something that big and noisy just disappear?

In an explosive, noisy burst, I blew out my breath in a gust. The combination of altitude, walking up hill, and terror played hell with holding my breath. I bent over gasping, feeling like I would never satisfy my lungs' demand for oxygen.

When I finally caught my breath, I searched through the leaves at my feet as quietly as I could in order to find my multi tool and extended the three-inch knife. Needless to say, it felt inadequate. Tommy should have given me something more than this "pocket utensil," but the government was very restrictive on personal weapons at that time, unless you were a jackass like Don, of course.

I had asked Tommy about getting a firearm, a machete or something, but he told me my first priority was to find a band of survivors and that they would take care of me. I then asked for advice if I ran into a zombie, and he told me that the area where I was headed was pretty much clear of zombies due to the rugged nature of the mountains, but I suspected him of lying especially after seeing some on the drive. When I pressed the issue of a zombie encounter, he simply told me to run to the nearest village. I hadn't thought to ask about what if I couldn't find a village. I had never considered the true expanse of the wilderness. All in all, I was under informed at best and lied to at worst.

I took a breath as if I was about to dive headfirst into a cold mountain spring and finally walked into the bush looking for whatever made the noise. I was scared, but it was even scarier not knowing what was pursuing me. I pushed my way through the branches and looked.

Nothing.

"Come out, you bastard," I demanded in a harsh whisper through clenched teeth. I searched the stand of bushes, my small knife leading my way like a flashlight. I was on a hair trigger.

I stepped on something round under the leaves. A head raised up three feet from me under the leaves ready to strike. It was surely the gray, spade shaped head of a giant rattlesnake.

I screamed, jumped back and fell on my butt due to the slope of the mountain. I kept screaming and kicking, trying to get away, trying to defend, trying to get to my feet, but all I could do was flail my legs. It was horrifying being on the ground with that snake. I finally calmed a bit as nothing attacked me. Maybe the snake had disappeared when I took my foot off of it.

I sat there for a moment to catch my breath. I told myself that it was winter and that snakes were hibernating. That didn't quell my fears much. There were so many rumors and conspiracy theories of new monsters that had been spawned in the Forbidden Zone. After all, a giant rattle snake that thrived in the winter was no less strange than a zombie or a vampire.

Again, curiosity got the best of me. I crawled forward, then stood and looked the place over. I saw nothing but a large tree branch.

I swore as I figured it all out: I simply stepped on one end of a branch. That caused the other end to rise. I looked at what I thought was the head of the rattlesnake. It was nothing but a misshapen piece of wood. It looked nothing like a snake. I cursed my overactive imagination and tried to calm myself.

However, I couldn't. I was still clueless as to what had originally made that loud crashing noise. I tried to convince myself that what I heard was an overactive imagination, such as mistaking a stick for a snake, but I knew that I did not imagine that thrashing through the leaves.

I swore again and told myself to get my act together. I found myself talking, mumbling to myself a lot on this hike. I kept forgetting that my recording devices were on and that I probably sounded crazy, but it became harder to talk to myself because I was constantly out of breath. So, my talking became breathless mutterings. As odd as it sounds, mumbling like a crazy man somehow kept me sane.

In the week before all this, I tried to get in shape by walking and jogging a few miles every day around the flat streets of DC. That was so naïve of me, but it was too late to do anything about my lack of conditioning now.

I kept trudging up the mountain. I probably climbed at a rate of less than a half mile an hour. It was only two miles to the top of the ridgeline, and that was my goal. However, I didn't take into account the steepness or the many obstacles. So many times, I had to stop, retrace my steps, and go around a rock formation, or I had to fight through a stand of thickets where I had to take off my pack to squeeze through a hole that seemed just big enough for a rabbit.

It was twilight when I finally reached the top of the ridgeline. It was topped with sharp rocks like the bony skeleton of a snake's vertebrae. I tried to look through the trees at that vantage point, but was disheartened to see no sign of humans. No people, old buildings, not even smoke from a campfire. Only miles of endless trees and hills. On a postcard it would have been breathtakingly gorgeous. The expanse of the valley, the ridgeline and peaks, I had only seen such scenery in pictures. Pictures that did real life no justice. Now, I could only offer curses to its solitude and beauty.

The beautiful warm sunny day had turned cold and dismal. I had not noted the change as I had trudged up the mountain. The altitude placed me right up there with the grey clouds. My hot, wet sweat suddenly felt like icy underground rivers running down the skin beneath my jacket. I started to shiver as I took off my backpack, and it immediately started to slide down the hill. As I reached for it, I slipped, fell and slid down the hill after my pack. The downward momentum of both myself and my pack was stopped suddenly by smacking into a thick tree.

I secured my backpack and looked below me. About twenty yards further down the slope was a drop-off into nothing. I eased down the hill restraining any further fall by grasping onto saplings until I stood on a precipice. It was about one hundred meters of a sheer drop down a granite cliff. I suffered a bit of vertigo as I looked at the jagged boulders down below that would savagely greet anyone unlucky enough to fall.

I sighed and scrambled back to the ridgeline, looking around for a relatively flat spot to put up my tent. However, there was no such thing as flat unless you pitched a tent for a creature the size of an ant.

"Screw it," I muttered.

The sun had set, so using the light from my headlamp, I pitched a tent on what felt like a 45-degree surface. I tried to follow the directions on the tent's package, but there was a big sag in the center of the tent, and I had a tent pole left over when I finished setting it up. One nice thing about solitude is that no one is there to see your follies. I then cursed the camera vest and cap and hoped I could delete the whole of today without anyone ever seeing the footage. I never wanted to see it, nor did I want anyone else, particularly Tommy, viewing my awkwardness.

I hadn't crossed the ridge to sleep. The rocky ridgeline felt like a wall between me and the unknown. Tomorrow, I would cross. Today I wanted to sleep on the same side where my friend Tommy dropped me off. I missed my home already and desperately.

I fumbled with a camp stove for a few minutes, but between my cold, numb fingers and lack of familiarity with the gadget, I soon gave up. Besides, my stomach was still too queasy to eat anything.

Instead, I pulled my sleeping bag out of my pack and brought it in the tent with me, leaving my gear outside. The pack had food and had the potential to attract all manner of critters including bears. I should have tied the pack up off the ground from a tree branch, but I was exhausted. I crawled into the tent and curled up trying to find warmth. I felt like a parrot whose owners had covered the cage with a hood to make the bird quiet. I found myself immediately falling asleep without electronic distractions.

Unfortunately, the night noises kept waking me up just as I would drift off. I heard the crashing through the leaves that had scared me earlier in the day and started to suspect that it was a quick, smaller creature rather than a man-sized zombie. However, until I knew exactly what caused the ruckus, it still scared me at the core. I guess it's the primitive fear of the unknown. The little bouts of noise and waking carried on annoyingly, but also harmlessly, However, three hours after sunset, I heard something that sent pure unabated terror to my heart.

I had just drifted back to sleep. Jennifer entered my mind. I can't remember what she said in my sleepy state, but I remember her radiant smile. I knew I was dreaming, but I felt like I was in my own bed. She soon began to morph and I could feel a foreign influence in my dreams. I watched as Jennifer turned into the vampiress that was on the footage and had haunted my earlier dreams. She seemed to be trying to warn me about something, but I just couldn't quite hear or understand her. For some reason I wasn't scared until I heard the crunch of leaves from the placing of a single large foot. The footsteps were not a part of my dreams. I was instantly awake.

The sound wasn't the scurrying or crashing through the leaves that I had been hearing all day. Instead, it was a cold, calculated single footstep in the leaves, followed by a pause and another single footstep. It was definitely human or something that once was. It had to be something at least as large as me. It was the exact same sound my footsteps made when I was trying to walk silently on the leaves, maybe heavier.

I could feel cold sweat instantly beading all over my skin as each slow stalking step, unmistakably sounded like it was getting closer. It stopped ten feet from my tent and I could hear it grunting as it rustled through something. I sat up quietly, holding my breath. I grabbed and opened my inadequate knife and picked up my head lamp without turning it on. I unzipped a small portion of the tent flap, flicked on the headlamp, and shone the light in the direction of the noise.

I groaned as I turned off the headlamp and zipped up the flap. It was a bear with its hind end towards me. I caught my breath and unzipped the flap again. I aimed my light on him again. It had to weigh at least twice as much as me.

"Damn," I swore under my breath. The bastard had literally ripped open the fabric of my backpack with its razor honed claws and was ransacking my food. The bear did it with such smugness, that it didn't even react to me shining a light on it. The thing was treating my food and my pack like he owned it.

I zipped the flap back up. The slight fabric of the tent flap felt as inadequate as my small knife, but I had something else for such an encounter. I felt around for the bear spray. Besides my multi tool knife, bear spray was my only weapon. I found it, and aimed it in the direction of the bear, double checking to make certain the nozzle wasn't pointed at me. I unzipped the flap, hesitated, and sprayed directly at the bear.

I instantly fell back, coughing in total agony. My eyes stung. I couldn't breathe. It felt like I inhaled the angry inhabitants of a hornets' nest. Despite not being able to breathe, I somehow managed to curse enough to make a sergeant in the Marine Corps blush.

It took a few minutes for me to get my reactions under control and be able to see again. I had a string of snot about three feet long hanging from my nose. As I wiped my hand across my face, it felt like a jelly fish slapped me. I looked at the flap and realized that I shot the bear spray straight into the mosquito netting.

Looking past the screen, the bear seemed completely oblivious to my plight. He just kept chowing down and scattering clothes, food wrappers, survival gear and camera equipment everywhere. I cursed him loudly, but he still kept eating, so I ineffectively kept cursing.

The bear pawed around some more and grunted. I guess he ran out of food because he finally turned around and confidently walked towards me. My angry curses turned to screams of horror. The bear stopped a few feet from me, within easy lunging distance and stood up on his hind legs. He looked to be about as tall as that 20 feet high electric fence. My screams turned to reverential swearing and then to prayers as he prepared to lunge, but instead he went back to all fours and wrinkled his nose.

I saw a stone fly out of nowhere and strike the bear. I tried to convince myself that I didn't see a thrown stone, because I didn't want to consider who or what had thrown the projectile. Besides, the bear seemed to have little interest in me.

With a snort, and a haughty throw of his snout, the bear casually turned and waddled away. The pepper spray offended the bear's sense of smell. I felt a bit of shame that my greatest method of self-defense was simply that the animal saw me as grotesquely inedible.

Once I felt sure that it was gone, I exited the tent that felt like the inside of ghost pepper. I enjoyed the feel of the cold air against my stinging skin. I poured some bottled water over my face. I breathed in the air like drinking water from a cold spring and breathed out feeling relaxed.

I suddenly looked over my shoulder and caught my breath. I could have sworn I saw the figure of a hooded, black cloaked being staring at me. I blinked and it stepped back into the gloom, but it was so faint to begin with that I doubted my sanity. Despite the billowing cloak, I was sure it was a willowy feminine form beneath. I thought of the vampiress.

I told myself that the bear spray had given me a nudge towards hallucinations, as I quickly scurried back into the tent.

I sat down into my sleeping bag and fell back into my pillow. I painfully tried to sleep after an hour with no further sign of the bear. It started to drizzle and then rain pretty hard. When I saw that there were no leaks in the tent, I relaxed. The rain had a calming effect on my nerves. I figured the bears and anything else would go back to their caves, dens, and lairs. Besides, I enjoyed how the rain would drown out the sound of anything walking in the woods. As silly as it sounds, I liked that because my nerves were frayed and even though most of what I heard was really nothing dangerous, the sound from the unknown creatures scared me. Also, at this point between the long day, constant terror, and lack of sleep from the last two nights, I really didn't care anymore. I just wanted oblivious repose.

I finally felt as if I was sinking into sleep. I dreamed I was sinking and then falling down into a black oblivion. I could feel the ground moving beneath me. My eyes widened as I realized I wasn't asleep or dreaming. I was actually sliding across the wet leaves.

The rain had made the leaves slippery and my tent had turned into a toboggan as I slid down the hill towards the edge of that cliff with the jagged rocks below. Each time I bounced off a tree or rock I could swear that I broke a bone. I tried to grab some handhold, whether a branch, rock or even dirt, but I was rolling helplessly ensconced in the tent and sleeping bag and couldn't actually grasp anything but the tent floor. Finally, I crashed face first into a tree and stopped.

I scrambled to find the zipper as the tent and I slowly started to slip around the tree toward the cliff's edge. I felt my legs dangle and slide off the abyss of the cliff.

"Please God! No!" I pleaded in panic. My hand found my knife and I sliced my way out as the tent kept sliding off the cliff. I finally got my hands out of the tent. I hugged the tree that had smashed my nose as my tent, sleeping bag, and everything else plummeted into the darkness below. I listened, but never heard my stuff hit bottom.

I cursed as I realized that I lost my flashlight.

Shaking with cold and fear, I scrambled back up to the backbone ridgeline and collapsed, leaning against a tree trunk, panting, exhausted, and beat up. I felt the rain on my face and to my list of miseries, I added soaking clothes whose damp coldness reached my marrow.

I laid down on the spot where I had put up my tent. The leaves were damp, but slightly less so where the tent had set. I got no rest before I sat up and felt around for my backpack to find a better coat, but it seemed that my pack slid down the cliff with my tent. I curled up under a tree and waited for the dawn that seemed as mythical as a fairy godmother.

***

I jolted awake. A pink line formed across the dark and distant jagged mountainous horizon, and I felt a small hope growing in my heart. As the eternal night had worn on, I really thought that the dawn would never arrive.

My teeth were chattering so loud with my shivering that I thought every zombie in the Forbidden Zone could hear the clicking. Actually, I was so miserable, that at the moment, that I scarcely feared anything, until I noticed I had a black cloak laying over me. There was a slight smell of the vampiress from the dreams, the same scent that I thought lingered in my bedroom after I woke up.

I swore and stood up with a bolt as I pushed the black cloak away, but I was alone and if folklore was to be believed, I need not worry about her or any vampires in the light of day.

Now that I could see and move without fear of falling off of the cliff, I saw that ice was starting to form on the leaves. As I looked closer, I could see that the cuffs on my pants were freezing as well. I picked up the vampiress' cloak and wrapped it around me for added warmth.

I walked to the edge of the cliff and saw my pack, tent, and supplies strewn about the jagged rocks far below.

"Oh my God!" I wasn't sure if there was a God or not in that miserable moment, but I said that as a prayer rather than an oath. God or not, at this point, I definitely believed in a hell. I now stood on hell's summit.

I quickly summed up my situation: I had no food, thanks to the bear. I had cut a hole in my tent so I had no shelter even if I could find it over the cliff. My clothes, as well as the mysterious black cloak, were soaked and it was below freezing. Any change of clothes was over the cliff and probably wet and torn from the bear ravaging claws. Anything I could use to light a fire was in my pack. I knew that I stood a good chance of slipping into hypothermia and dying in these wet and frigid conditions. And I didn't know where the band of survivors lived who I was seeking for safety.

I collapsed in a seated position and fought against weeping. I was a failure. I had no hope but to abandon my adventure if I wished to live. It is embarrassing to admit to almost crying, but this was just a long string of failures in my life. I would be a laughing stock, and this had been my last chance at something better. It was my chance to prove the world wrong.

Driven by my physical discomfort, the chance of dying in the elements, and hitting another wall of failure, I found myself asking: what was the point of living if I had failed at this latest endeavor, not even twenty-four hours into the mission? This was just another disappointment of many notched into my skull.

I eased my way down to the edge of the cliff and looked over the ledge. I crept over more so that I stood over a line of jagged boulders far beneath me. I held my breath as something in the darkest recesses of my soul contemplated a jump. It was a brief, but horrific flight of fancy. I pushed it from my mind and told myself that most likely a suicide attempt would not be instant. Instead, my shattered body would probably just lie on the sharp boulders as I awaited something to come out of the woods and devour me. Or, I would get bit, turned into a zombie and lie there unable to move in unnatural life for eternity. Even as a zombie, I'd be a failure. This made me chuckle in morbid humor. I was losing my mind.

I sat on the precipice and wallowed in my insanity as the tarnished, dime sized winter sun stoically rose above me. How long did I stay? I could not tell. The red dawn light that colored my surroundings slowly turned orange and then a tarnished silvery white. I sat there now numb to my shivering. It annoyed me that I had those suicidal thoughts even for a moment. I could be impulsive but that new and sudden impulse worried me.

No, I told myself. I had to find my pack and continue somehow. I still had my body cam. I must make it work. I needed a documentary. I was here.

Something deep inside me, that I didn't know that I had, propelled me to stand and walk, first around the precipice of course and then downhill. I needed my backpack with a change of clothes.

I followed the ledge until I came to a more gradual slope. I recognized a rock formation that looked like an old bearded man contemplating the seeming eternity of the mountains. On the way down, I mostly slipped on the icy leaves, fell and caught myself on the closest tree trunk or branch. I would let go of the branch, slip, fall, catch myself again and repeat and repeat. I went into a trance in this manner and lost track of where I was. I soon became numb to the thrashing I received from plummeting through trunks and branches.

I had no idea where my pack would be. I had trouble forming thoughts. I was dying of exposure, I slowly and dumbly realized. My clothes were still coated in ice. I unconsciously resigned myself to the failure of the mission and simply stumbled downhill to the fence and my way out of this mess. I wanted a hot, hot, very hot cup of coffee more than anything in the world. I didn't care if it was 99.9% cut by dandelion roots either. Without my gear, I realized I had to return to civilization. I had to sneak across the fence in order to survive.

A drone checked me out for a moment hovering just out of arm's reach. The camera head of it cocked back and forth like a child pondering if a goofy uncle was a good or bad guy. I had a flash of annoyance, but then the drone seemed to be a companion of sorts. I tried talking to it, because I was tiring of mad conversations with myself, but it cocked itself again and flew away. Apparently, I was not that interesting.

It was noon when I stumbled up to the fence. I would have hugged it, but I remembered the razor wire and the raging electricity. I looked, and fifty yards away to my left was the rock formation with the boulder doing the balancing act over the area that hid the steel pipe that would lead me to freedom.

I was grateful for easily finding it. It wasn't woodsmanship or even dumb luck. Yesterday, I had simply walked uphill against gravity. Today, I had simply followed gravity by falling back to where I started, but somehow it seemed that the downhill walk (controlled fall) wore me out more than the uphill climb.

I made my way to the pipe and slumped to the ground and slithered into the hole. I didn't try too hard to cover the back entrance. I didn't care about anything other than getting back to my real life and accepting a fate of a life with no ambitions.

"Hot coffee," I said to encourage myself as I crawled through the freshly spun spider webs and dirt in the pipe.

I pushed the sticks and leaves out of my way to exit, and climbed out. I stood up brushing spider webs and other debris off my body. I looked straight ahead thinking of my next move, but instead, I stared straight into three gun barrels. Behind the three armed soldiers in biohazard suits, sat a five-gallon gas can for my imminent funeral pyre. I closed my eyes and awaited the impact of the bullets.

| 8 |

Too many moments passed without feeling the bullets ravage me. I opened my eyes and stared into the emotionless goggle eyes of the armed soldiers' shiny black biohazard masks. The filters were located in the beak-like area of the front. It was obviously in the style of the birdlike masks from the plagues of the Dark Ages. On TV, the characters wearing them struck me as cartoonish. Seeing them up close with firearms aimed at me froze my heart. The glassy eyes of the gas mask got to me the most. It was like meeting three Darth Vaders. I closed my eyes again and waited for the impact of the bullets.

And waited.

What the hell? I thought. These storm troopers were facing a firing squad as well if they didn't shoot me on the spot. I could swear that I heard their fingers creaking on the triggers.

I heard one of them say in a youthful high-pitched voice, "Shoot him, man."

Another one whined, "No, you first."

I uncoiled from my cowering stance and looked closer at them. The guns were shaking slightly in their adrenalized hands. I could see just enough behind the goggles that these were eighteen, maybe nineteen, year old kids. Probably just last year they were trying to figure out how to get a cheerleader in the backseat of their car without a clue of what to do next with her. These weren't killers, at least not yet.

I stood to my full height and forced my shoulders back in a false display of confidence. "Good morning, Marines." I didn't know what they were, but I knew that Marines got mad if you called them soldiers, but not the other way around. Besides, I thought I would flatter them. "I am on a secret mission with direct orders from your boss Senior Deputy Thomas Laurens, and ultimately from my uncle, Governor Daniel Hildebrande."

I felt my desperation as I name dropped. Almost like a man in the movies will hold a cross and speak sacred names to a vampire, but luckily it seemed to be working for me. All three men lowered their guns, mere inches, but it was a start.

I laid the BS on thick. They looked back and forth to each other as they tried to follow my story. It wasn't really a story; I just said whatever popped into my head to stall the inevitable. I figured when I stopped talking, they'd shoot.

Finally, one of them said in a modulated voice through his mask, "OK, OK man. We'll take you back to headquarters. Just shut up for now."

They slowly lowered their rifles a little more. However, now they aimed the barrels at my crotch instead of my chest. Having a gun pointed at the groin isn't pleasant from a physical standpoint, but I knew I was getting through to them. In fact, from that point onward, I had a gun constantly pointed at me for the next hour or so. That does wear on the psyche in a way I can't explain. I was literally under the gun.

In the robotic voice modulated by the face mask, I heard one of them ask, "Governor Daniel Hildebrande sent you?"

I straightened and despite my fear, or maybe because of my fear, I knew if I didn't put on a show of confidence, I would be immediately shot, incinerated, and my ashes scattered. I took on an air of command, and acted like my friend Tommy.

"Yes. My Uncle Dan, Governor Hildebrande to you, sent me on this mission. It's also a secret operation, and I can't say anything more." In retrospect, that lie was comical in the fact that I had just blabbed a whole load of crap about my supposed mission in the moments before.

They all put a hand to their left shoulders and seemed to look at each other for a few minutes. I later learned that their left shoulder had a button that allowed them to communicate with each other without me overhearing.

They finally pushed me ahead with their rifle tips, afraid to even touch me with their protective gloves. They ordered me into the back of a Humvee that was manufactured like a pickup truck. I sat on the hard metal floor of the back bed, but it felt comfortable just to get off of my feet and away from the forest floor. I leaned back and then I almost screamed as I realized I was leaning against a gas can. The realization that I came in contact with the canister that held the fuel for burning my dead remains horrified me to the core.

When we arrived back at an outpost, a man in a biohazard suit and bird beaked mask stopped the vehicle with an authoritatively raised hand. By his posture, I could tell that he was not going to be a pushover like my three captors.

The driver slammed on the breaks. "Yes, Sergeant?" he asked as they all stepped out of the vehicle. I joined them now with four guns pointed at me.

The three men who had captured me received an ass-chewing that made me cringe. I was sure that they would face the firing squad that I was supposed to face. After chewing them out, the Sergeant turned his Darth Vader goggled eyes towards me.

"Get your ass over here!" he barked.

I obeyed the order, and he pulled a handgun and placed it against my head. He explained to the kids who captured me, "This is how you shoot an outlander. Get the gas can."

I tried to use the magic words again, "But Governor Hildebrande is my--"

"Shut up!"

He pulled the trigger. I heard a click and cringed. The sergeant cursed, worked the slide to chamber around and aimed at my head again. My legs gave out, and I fell on my knees.

The Sergeant hesitated as a black Mercedes with opaque and mirrored windows flew straight at us. I thought I would die by the impact of a car versus a bullet, but it came to a screeching, grinding halt on the gravel road, the bumper lightly tapped my face. I heard the car door open and slam and running footsteps coming up to us, as I coughed on the dust that the vehicle stirred.

I could hear the fear in the Sergeant's voice as he said, "Sir, we are just executing— "

I peeked through squinted eyes to see Don towering above us all. He inspired the same terror, maybe more, into the Sergeant as he did with me. Don said, "You've done well, Sergeant. I'll handle this from here."

Don turned his cold mackerel eyes toward me. He had his own handgun pointed at my head. I saw the faintest hint of a smile as he turned the gun from me and shot the sergeant dead center in the chest.

I saw the Sergeant look at him with the mortal knowledge that he was dying that second. His mouth opened as if to ask the existential question, "Why?" but no words came out. He was dead as he hit the ground.

Don pumped another bullet into his head.

Don turned to the three remaining soldiers who were fearfully backing up, "Stand still."

They obeyed him out of terror. After he calmly shot two of them, the remaining one turned to run. Don's shot caught him in the back of the head. The man collapsed.

The gun circled back to me.

I was too numb with shock to even cry out. He lowered his gun to his side. "Move the bodies off the road where they can't immediately be seen. Move! Now!" He roared the last two words.

I just looked at him, too shocked to move. The violence I had witnessed could torment people for years. I only had a few seconds to appreciate what I saw and could only respond by staring with horror. I was in so far over my head that I could only stare stupidly at him and mutter, "Please, Please. I am sorry."

Don pushed me over with a shoving foot on my shoulder and then kicked me in the side as hard as he could. "Move when I say, 'Move!' Damn it!"

I moved and grabbed the boots of one of the dead men. His mask had flown off of him when Don's bullet shattered his head. His uniform was covered in his own brain matter. Don picked up his phone and made a call. "Yes, he is alive, although barely through my good graces." He gave me a dirty look and walked out of my hearing range.

I went back to work hauling the bodies. I never realized how heavy a dead person was until then. I had also never seen a freshly shot dead person close up before. The terror was etched on their faces. The mortal questions blazed in their eyes beneath the slowly glazing and glassed over surfaces. There was an ickiness to even touching them as their muscles had no reaction or resistance to my handling. That was layered with the fear that I wasn't far from joining them.

When I finally moved the last body just out of sight, Don walked straight up to me. From the quick and sure swing of his long stride, I thought he was going to punch me or shoot me. Instead he grabbed my hair and pulled me towards the outpost.

"Aren't you afraid that I may have some of the germs from the Forbidden Zone?" I asked, hoping he'd let go.

Instead, he grabbed my hair tighter, smacked me hard across the face, and growled, "Shut up."

We entered the drab military bunker that was just large enough for an office with two small jail cells. He threw me in a cell by my hair, but he didn't bother to close or lock the cell. This actually confused me.

So, I asked, "Aren't you afraid that I'll try to escape?"

He ignored me and made a snorting sound that may have been the closest thing he had to a laugh. He sat down and placed his feet on the lone desk and read a magazine that was on the top.

"Hey thanks for saving me," I said. I knew that it sounded lame, but I wanted him to say something that would give me a hint of what was going on.

He placed down the magazine and looked at me with his fish cold eyes, "You are only alive because my orders are not to kill you, yet. If my orders come down to kill you, you will be dead. Nothing you say will change it or gain you any extra time. However, I can kick your ass all I want in the meantime, so I suggest that you not piss me off. In other words, shut the hell up."

He calmly went back to reading his magazine without waiting for me to respond.

I looked at my hands, which were shaking like I suffered from palsy. No matter what I did, they wouldn't stop trembling from the adrenalin dump.

An hour passed and Tommy arrived. He actually looked unfazed like everything was in control and had happened according to plan. "Hey, Don," he said like he was walking into the office on a normal business day.

Tommy did a double take when he looked at my face. He greeted me with, "Holy hell. You look like crap. Your face! Are you alright, Eric?"

"Sure. A little rattled, but I am fine," I said putting on a brave face.

"Your face," Tommy repeated.

I was about to ask what he meant, but when I curiously touched my face, I winced from the pain and realized I must have appeared badly bruised from the falls I took. In fact, I could see the bruise on the bridge of my nose when I crossed my eyes. I kept thinking I had a bug or a smudge of dirt on it. I guess it was from the face plant into the tree as I sledded down the hill in the tent.

"Did your captors do this to you?" he asked.

I looked to Don to see if he was fearful that I might tell on him, but he had no worries.

"No, Don was kind to me," I said, still trying to get in his good graces.

Don showed no emotions and kept reading the magazine.

Tommy nodded and said, "It must have been the fall down the cliff."

I looked at him and the sudden movement hurt my neck. "How did you know that I fell?"

"Suspicious, aren't you?" Tommy laughed. "When a city boy such as yourself ventures into the mountains, he's bound to fall. It was as certain as you screwing up this assignment, but I figured that you'd last longer than 24 hours. Why didn't you try to find the survivors after you lost all your gear?"

"How did you know that I lost my gear?" I asked. I suspected that they were watching me the whole time. Now I knew for sure. It irked me that my friend still denied it, like I was out of their circle. I realized I would always be on the outs.

He looked at me like I was a complete idiot. "You came back with no gear, correct?" He took a deep breath and looked past me, and with hands raised toward the heavens, he acted like he was asking the universe for advice. "Now, what are we going to do with you?"

The way he said that chilled me to the bone. It was obvious that he had very little say in the matter and like Don, that he was resigned to follow whatever orders came down the chain.

Just then Tommy's phone rang. His eyes widened slightly as he looked at who was calling him.

He held up a finger to me and said, "Hold on a moment," without looking in my direction.

He stepped outside the small building, but didn't bother to close the door.

"Good morning, sir," Tommy said into the phone as he looked at the screen. There were only a handful of people who he had to address as sir. I shuddered. After a pause, he said, "Yes. He screwed up again, this time very royally, but we expected that. I think your plan is sound, sir."

Don snorted from the corner, but kept reading his magazine.

After a brief conversation on the phone out of my earshot, Tommy walked back in and held up the screen for me to talk.

My blood ran cold as I looked at the screen and saw the stern, officious face. "Uncle Dan..." I exclaimed

"That's Governor to you." He then proceeded to curse me with words that would have shocked his constituents. Although he didn't actively court the rightwing religious votes that much, he still paid Christianity some lip service because most of the people in his area claimed that religion. However, I had a feeling that if overnight the Wiccan beliefs became the dominant religion in his region, he would go on TV with a newly purchased broom and a black pointy hat if that's what he thought was required to garner the votes to keep him in power.

He vented his wrath at me for a minute or so until I got irritated enough to say, "Hey Gov, I just watched your errand boy, Don, murder four people in cold blood. Your yelling hardly fazes me at this point. Just tell me my fate."

He glared at me through the screen for a moment, took a deep breath as if he was about to really excoriate me for another minute, but instead chose a schmaltzier tactic. Rather than screaming, he sighed and said, "Eric, I raised you like a son after your parents passed away. I've helped you the best I could with all your hair brained schemes, hoping that you'd be at least half the man that my brother, your father, was. Now this? You really should be dead, but for my mercy."

I was exhausted and shell-shocked. I really had no care left to give. I was aware that they already knew my fate. I simply wanted to know the outcome as well. Was I going to jail? Was I just going back to my normal life? Was this moment my last to live? "Cut the crap, Gov! I'm not dead. If I should be, I would be." I saw Don look at me with surprise and he actually smirked with a hint of admiration. I finished my rant, "Just tell me what's up."

My Uncle sighed and acted like a governor again. Any familial love was gone. He spoke more like an impartial judge rather than an angry uncle, "Tommy, Don," he said, "Carry out the plan of the day."

Tommy nodded and said, "Yes sir," and took his phone back from my hand. His brown eyes were as dead as mud puddles. I heard Don actually laugh as a black cloth sack was pulled over my head. Don slammed me against the desk and expertly handcuffed me before I realized what was happening. He smacked me across the head as I feebly resisted.

| 9 |

After getting blinded by the hood and shackled, Don pushed me out the door of the building. I could hear the heavy thumping of a helicopter heading in our direction.

"Is that bird for me?" I asked.

"Shut up," Don said.

"Tommy?" I yelled.

"Sorry, Eric. This is the best deal that I could get you."

I was worried that I would cry, but I kept relatively calm as I asked. "Am I going to live?" My voice cracked slightly.

"That's entirely up to you." Don said without mercy. "You can't fight worth a damn, so I suggest you work on your BSing skills. You are now permanently an outcast."

An icy hand seemed to grip me and squeeze every last bit of hope from my body and soul.

When I said nothing, Don added with a cruel chuckle, "Yep. You wanted to make a name for yourself, well here's your chance."

"Take the hood off, Don." Tommy ordered with a hint of compassion.

Don complied without question. Although once the hood was off, I could see in his face he didn't like the order.

Tommy looked me in the eyes. I could see something that resembled concern or friendship. "You're getting flown back out there. You'll have all the filming and computers and solar rechargers needed," Tommy said. "The Governor wanted you dead, but here you get a chance at a reprieve. I'll keep working through the channels. Maybe in a year or two things will change enough and we'll get you out."

Don held on like he expected me to collapse from fear, but I was beyond that. I said, "A year or two? I barely survived eighteen hours! I am a dead man! You know it. Please, just let me sneak back. I would rather live as an anonymous homeless bum in DC than out in those woods. Please."

Tommy raised his voice to speak over the helicopter that was now hovering over the trees and starting to land in a nearby clearing, "The chopper will take you within a few miles of a settlement."

"A few miles? How will I find them?" I asked having already spent a day wandering a few miles.

"I'm sure they will find you," Don interjected with his chuckle. As things became more intense, he seemed to actually smile.

Tommy nodded, "They are very aware of intruders."

"I don't want to be an intruder." I said as the helicopter landed. Tommy stopped following us and stood watching as

Don pushed my head down and ducked to avoid decapitation by the rotor blades.

"That's where your gift of bull comes in," Don shouted as we arrived at the chopper. He guided me in, pushed me through the cargo door and then shouted in my ear once we were both inside. "Oh yeah, so you can't try to wander back again."

I was plunged into darkness as the hood was slammed over my head once more. As we walked the final steps to the bird, Tommy yelled at me over the noise explaining that my mission was the same, to get some good footage and stories.

In the blackness of the hood, Don guided me and boarded the chopper with me.

***

The flight wrenched my gut. For one thing, it was my first ride in a Blackhawk helicopter, but on top of that, I experienced the changes of gravity with a blindfold over my eyes. It sucked. I dry heaved a bit and realized that I hadn't eaten in over a day. I was grateful that I had nothing to upchuck into the black hood. That would have been plain nasty.

After fifteen minutes flying, Don pulled the hood off of my head. I blinked a few times as I got used to the light.

A soldier in a biohazard suit and one of the bird masks manned a pretty heavy looking machine gun that pointed out the cargo door. His goggled eyes peered out over the terrain and had no interest in me. The pilots were unseen behind a cabin wall.

I had read that Blackhawk helicopters can fly over a hundred and fifty miles an hour. I guessed that I was at least 30 miles from the border. Having covered barely two miles on the mountainous terrain on foot, I knew that sneaking back was not an immediate option, especially considering that I had no idea which direction to head.

Don took off the handcuffs and handed me a pair of headsets. I placed them on. He then handed me the handcuffs with the keys. I could hear his voice clearly through the ear pieces, "Keep the cuffs. You might be able to use them as barter. It's a different world down there."

I pocketed the cuffs and the keys.

He spoke to me for a few minutes sharing some survival tips and ideas to deal with the locals. He actually seemed fairly fatherly in his advice as if he truly wanted me to succeed. He told me that Tommy would send a drone out on occasion to pick up the computer chip with the footage that I recorded as well as dropping off gifts for me. That would be the extent of our communication.

He specifically warned me not to approach a drone that didn't approach me. Don told me that in order to prevent capture, they had enough explosives to level a house.

I nodded and worried about any drone that got near me after that.

As he spoke, I kept my mouth shut to avoid angering him. I still suspected that there was a chance they might throw me out of the chopper from a few thousand feet above the ground. I had seen that when I did some reporting in South and Central America.

I did speak up as I noticed a large gathering of people crammed together in a valley. There had to be thousands maybe tens of thousands. It looked like it had to be some kind of outdoor music concert in the way they were packed together. However, I suspected that the gathering was anything but fun. There was something sinister in the way they moved slowly with occasional spastic jerks.

"What's that?" I asked Don. "A music festival," I forced a joke. Humor seemed to be my go-to in times of stress.

"Nope, those are the zombies. Some of them"

I swore. Just the magnitude of monstrous humanity froze me to the core. Seeing it in real life was a heavy weight to bear.

I asked Don, "Why are they crammed together?"

"They have a herd instinct, like your average human voter. They probably still chant the names of their favorite politicians," Don snorted cynically as if he was someone who was above the laws, politicians, and other quirks of humanity.

"Why are they in the valley?"

Don explained, "They devoured everything in the towns and are looking for food, people, elsewhere. However, they take the paths of least resistance. They won't venture off the roads unless they smell or hear something that promises easy access to food. Again, humanity hasn't changed."

"What attracts them?" I asked.

"Anything. Everything," He said studying the ground below with an eye that held no fear. "Sounds. Gunshots especially. They can hear those from miles away and it promises that something is wounded and an easy dinner. That's why so many people use swords, machetes, clubs, and bows and arrows. Besides, after two years, bullets are scarcer than tits on a bull."

Once we flew over a ridge and I couldn't see the zombies anymore, I quit talking to Don. It was depressing how little faith he had in humanity. It was even more depressing because I suspected that he may be correct. He was so high up in the secret workings of government, he had to know so much and yet he was by far the most cynical bastard I had ever met. I prayed that it was more of his nature rather than what he actually knew.

I felt a dread come over me as the helicopter slowed and started to descend. The floor of the helicopter would be my last contact with civilization, indefinitely.

Don paternally slapped me on the back. "You'll do fine, kid."

He took the headphones off my head and said gently, "Alright. Get going. Some people are on the way to pick you up."

In a small clearing, the helicopter lowered to a few feet off the ground as if afraid of making physical contact with the land for fear of contracting the zombie disease.

I hesitated.

"Get going," he repeated not quite as gently.

"I can't," I said truthfully. My feet would not move. I did not want to break from my last contact with civilization. The cold realization that there was no going back slammed hard.

I suddenly found myself flying out of the large cargo door and realized that Don had literally booted me out. I fell six feet to the rocky mountain soil. I barely rolled out of the way as a huge backpack followed me and landed where I had just fallen. I looked closer and saw that it was the exact same pack that had fallen off the cliff. I could even see scratches from the damn bear that had been stitched up and repaired with rubberized patches. It was heavily re-stuffed gear. Earlier, Don said it had more survival stuff and things to barter to ingratiate me into my new tribe. I had all the proof that this outcome had been planned all along. There was nothing I could do, but my best.

I looked at Don. Again, I flipped him the finger. The Darth Vader like door gunner showed no emotion. Don actually smiled. I could barely hear him over the thumping rotor wash, but through the help of lip reading I could tell that he said, "You're the one who's screwed."

Even as they flew away, the door gunner kept the barrel aimed at me.

I actually felt tears threatening to spill as the finality settled on my shoulders. This scheme that I dreamed up, the one that was supposed to help me live my life to my full potential, had in effect just ended it. I pushed my self-pity aside. I had to start thinking like a survivor and also like a journalist. Not just my immediate survival, but my documentation would give me a bit of immortality.

But first I had to survive.

For a moment however, I stood watching the chopper leave. Anger replaced my fear once I was beyond the range of the machine gun, then a numbness hit as the Blackhawk formed a soundless black dot on the horizon. I felt the darkest, hopeless doom. It was when both the sight and sound of the helicopter were gone that the oppressive reality hit me. They weren't coming back. I should have done something worth getting shot over, but again I realized this exile was all planned in advance. Only three people knew about my crime of crossing the border and they all had prior knowledge of the plan. This exile was not out of mercy.

Even though I had my livelihood in the backpack, everything I needed for making a documentary, even if it was the most kick ass documentary ever, I would never get to enjoy the rewards in a civilized world. Tommy was lying when he said that he would get me a reprieve in a year or so. I knew it. I was officially dead. I just didn't eat the brains of the living like real zombies, at least not yet. Still, I was not ready to die yet. I had to survive.

Things chirped, critters noisily shuffled through the leaves, the wind howled, unknown rustlings and screechings. I even thought I heard some very distant mocking laughter. However, I had a hard time hearing between my thundering heartbeat, rapid breathing, and my feet crunching on the leaves as I kept looking for the sources of the noises, spinning in a circle on the forested mountain top like a demented scene from the Sound of Music. I was later told that's what I indeed looked like.

I finally caught my breath and quit moving for a moment and just listened. Somewhere in my mind, I knew that what I was hearing was a large animal. It wasn't just a rustling through the leaves. Rather it was a singular, heavy crunch of leaves. Then a brief pause and another, "crunch." Like the night before when I heard the bear approach my tent. I could feel my skin get a cold sweaty sheen as I turned to look. I didn't have my bear spray handy.

I jumped, screamed, and fell to the ground when I heard something whistle over my head and saw an antlerless deer shoot away through the woods. An arrow shot over its back. I lay there looking to my left as it disappeared.

I then whipped my head to my right as I heard the noisy thrashing through the leaves like I did the day before when I couldn't find the source. I screamed again as a squirrel charged straight to my face. The animal stopped inches away. It stared at me in shock and ran the other way in a bolt of brown and red fur. I screamed again and jumped to my feet.

I realized that the mysterious terror of the day before was simply a squirrel. That is what made the thrashing sound in the leaves. I felt like a dunce.

I was about to breathe a sigh of relief, but I caught my breath as I remembered the errant arrow that had whistled above my head. That was when I heard the laughter of two men who sounded uncannily close by. I wheeled back to the direction I was just facing and there they were sitting on a log casually observing me from forty meters.

They were dressed in a mix of brown buckskin and camouflage. It appeared that they weren't hiding. I had just been too panicked to see what was in front of me earlier. So that as they sat still in their outdoorsy clothes, they were all but invisible to me until they wished to be seen.

They stood up still laughing. Each held a homemade longbow. With the laughter, archery stuff, and woodsy clothes, I may have confused them with Robin Hood's Merry Men, were it not for the anachronistic assault rifles strapped to their shoulders, ready for emergencies, and their eyes which were not merry. Yes, the corners of their eyes crinkled with laughter, but something beyond their pupils told a different story. Looking deep into their eyes, I could tell these were killers. They may not have been as evil as Don, but two years in the rough, the windows to their soul told me that they had had to kill to survive.

One was a short almost fat man (fat for the quarantined area), about fifty-five years old. He wore a ball cap in a crooked manner on his head. Not like a hipster trying to be cool, but rather like a redneck who just didn't care what people thought of him. He placed a baseball bat over one shoulder and set down his longbow. He had a beard about halfway down his chest. He laughed, and took off his cap. He ran his hand over his bald head as if somehow that would get him to regain his composure. It didn't. I later learned that his name was Scott. I don't think he was actually related to anyone in the tribe, but they referred to him as Uncle Scott nonetheless.

Scott said in a thick accent, "Damn son, I ain't never saw someone so scared of their dinner." The accent wasn't quite the lofty and beautiful southern drawl. It was similar in some ways but harsher, like the black sheep of a family.

The shock of numbness began to leave me. I felt my anger arising, but told myself to keep it in check so my impulsive nature didn't get me killed. I took him to be a dumbass with his thick accent, which sounded foreign to my North East Coast ears. Having a dumbass speak down to me is probably my biggest pet peeve.

However, the AK-47 slung over his back scared the hell out of me. It wasn't so much the gun; it was his casual acquaintance with it. The military police, who escorted me, carried theirs with a tension that screamed anger and fear. Yet this guy didn't seem to have a care in the world. I had the feeling he could draw the weapon, shoot me and not even pause in his laughter, but thankfully he didn't seem inclined.

The other man was tall, lean, mid-thirties, longish hair, and a short beard. I did a double take. He kind of looked like that father on that drone footage I watched back in the bar. If the man in the video hadn't surely met his death, I may have seriously thought it was him. However, this guy didn't have that determined look. He looked like some mellow hippy, but I guess most of the people out here looked like this due to the lack of hygiene and beauty salons. He had a black assault rifle strapped over his back. I later learned it was an AR-15. A katana sword was sheathed at his side.

The hippy just nodded his head as a response to Scott's laughter. I later learned that the hippy's name was Bryan.

"Do you men live around here?" I asked.

"Nope," said Bryan. Even with his monosyllabic speech, he didn't seem to have any accent I could pinpoint.

"Really?" I asked curiously.

"No," said the short fat one in one of the worst imitations of a New York accent ever, "A fricking helicopter just dropped us off too like it did with youse."

Both men laughed again. They then approached me casually. It reminded me of a video from a safari in Africa. I saw three lions confidently approach a cape buffalo in an almost friendly yet playful manner. They circled it and within a minute they were devouring the poor animal alive.

"Who are you guys?" I demanded.

"No," Bryan said. "Who are you to come into our land? Why is a man who is scared of squirrel and deer, made an outcast to the civilized world?"

"I'm Eric Hildebrande. I got caught sneaking into the," I hesitated to call their home the Forbidden Zone. I eventually just said, "Zone."

"Hildebrande, like the Governor Peckerhead," said Scott. He had a way of saying everything in a tone as if it were a joke. Usually just crudely calling someone a peckerhead would have had no effect on me, but even in the circumstance I found something funny about him. Had the circumstances been different, I may have laughed aloud.

Scott continued, "No wonder you ain't shot."

"This isn't punishment. I am a journalist," I stated. It wasn't the truth, but I wasn't going to appear like a victim.

"Of course," said Bryan dismissively. "What happened to your face?"

I remembered how bruised it was, so I thrust my chest out and boldly stated, "You should see the other guy's face."

Scott laughed and gently pushed me aside. He and Bryan, without asking and with the casualness of the lions, tore through my backpack. Actually, it was more like the bear from the night before, except they unbuttoned and unzipped rather than ravaged my pack with taloned claws. I felt just as powerless as I did last night, especially without the bear spray.

After a moment, I grew angry enough at the careless way they threw my stuff all over the place, and I stepped forward to stop them but Bryan looked at me and shook his head. There was no threat, no words, in fact he smiled in a friendly manner. The head shake seemed to imply without saying aloud, "We both know you don't have the balls to stop me."

I gritted my teeth knowing he was right.

"What the hell is all this?" demanded Scott. He held up a telescopic lens that was over twelve inches long and looked through it, "Daggum! This is almost as big as my pecker."

Bryan looked at me with a hint of concern. "You won't last a day out here, man. You have little food, no weapons— "

"I have this knife." I said holding up the multi-tool with the three-inch blade.

"'bout the size of your pecker," Scott laughed.

Bryan rolled his eyes as if his pecker was the only topic of conversation that Scott engaged in. He then looked pointedly at me, "Dude, they set you up to die."

"My mission is to meet up with a group of people like yourself and film how you survive. Like the reality show, Survivor Man or something."

"That's been done to death, even before all this went down," Bryan said with a hint of sympathy. "I don't think this will be as glamorous as you appear to think."

"Yeah, but what you do is real. I mean, picture it." I knew it looked cheesy, but I was desperate as I held both thumbs and forefingers up in a rectangle like a television and said, "You're doing something like lighting a fire—Yeah, been done to death-- but then just as the viewers get bored, a zombie attacks." I know what I did sounds melodramatic, but I was hoping these people with such little hope would be bedazzled. I was counting on being the savior to give some meaning to their lives.

Scott laughed hysterically, "That's gotta be the stupidest thing I done heard of."

I had a feeling Scott purposefully spoke horrible grammar for shock value. Everything about him seemed to be an act to get a rise out of someone. I couldn't tell if I found him to be annoying or funny. Maybe a little of both and that's probably why I wasn't sure.

Bryan casually leaned against a tree with a sad smile that showed that he was acting polite, but that he fully agreed with what Scott had said.

"Oh, crap," I exclaimed as I saw a human form lurching towards us. Scott and Bryan had their backs to the thing. Its putrid flesh was falling off of it and I could catch a faint scent of the decaying humanity. I could see the muscles of the face where the skin had fallen away as well as a few molars. Were it clothed, I would not have been able to tell that it was a male, but even that member was probably days away from completely falling off from rot.

"What's the matter?" asked Bryan.

The horror of it overwhelmed my nervous system and all could say was literally, "Wuh wuh," as I pointed.

"Son, what in the holy hell is a 'wuh wuh'?" asked Scott.

I muttered some more unintelligible syllables. The monster was ten feet behind them.

In seemingly a single motion, Bryan lazily leaned forward to get his back off the tree, turned to face the zombie, and drew his sword slicing the zombie's head off. It happened so fast that I stood staring for a moment as I digested what I had just witnessed.

As soon as the headless thing hit the ground, Bryan pulled out a cloth and an unlabeled plastic water bottle. He then wiped down his sword using a brownish liquid from the water bottle that I took to be an antiseptic. It smelled something like Listerine except a little more astringent.

"I was wondering when he'd get here," Bryan said with a bored voice.

Scott chimed in, "These rotters, like this headless guy here, are probably days away from falling apart. They don't move so fast."

"Yeah," Bryan agreed. "We saw him standing against a tree in sleep mode."

Scott looked at Bryan and said, "And he would have stayed that way if idiot here didn't wake him up with that damn whirly bird. By the way, nimrod, next time you see a zombie, don't say 'wuh wuh,' say, `Hey guys, there's a zombie behind you.'"

Now that the immediate danger was behind me, I realized that I needed these two. I could not spend the night alone in the woods and expect to survive without them. "So, what about the documentary?" I asked. "Interested?"

"And what in the holy hell do we get out of it?" demanded Scott with a mocking laugh.

"You get your name out there, to the public, your public." I answered, but saw that it wasn't selling. I put on a cheesy showman's voice and dramatically spread my arms for a comical effect. "Fame, fortune, you can keep up with the Kardashians?" I added as a joke.

They looked at me confused. Finally, Scott asked, "The Kar-what-in-the-hells?"

Bryan shook his head, "Sorry bro, this isn't going to work. You'll most likely be dead by morning anyway, so we'll just take your food," Bryan said motioning to my pack as if it were already a done deal.

"What? The hell you will," I said more in panic than anger.

"You done scared that deer and caused us to miss the shot," Scott explained. "That was our tribe's dinner tonight. Bryan's gots kids to feed. You owe us, peckerhead."

"Besides," Bryan added. "I highly suspect you as a spy with all that recording equipment."

Bryan and Scott started pocketing my camping food.

"Who the hell would want to spy on a bunch of hillbillies?" I asked. It wasn't a nice thing to say. I later learned that hillbilly is similar to the n- word in these mountains. However, in the moment, my emotions had taken over my reason.

Scott barely spoke between his chortling, "Some loser trash who society bashed his face up and discarded from a whirly bird, obviously."

That was like a hot iron spike driven into my chest. I felt an impulsive rage wash over me. They could insult me, but they couldn't steal all that I had left.

Bryan could see it. He smirked at me. I could tell that he was purposely pressing my buttons. It worked.

My grip tightened on my small knife and I charged at Bryan. Although I had some training in martial arts, I was fueled by pure brainless rage and desperation. Bryan calmly stepped aside and kicked my foot out as I barreled past him. I sprawled onto the leafy forest floor and lost my knife.

I sprang to my feet and charged again, swinging my fist at his smug face. Bryan easily ducked the blow. I saw a smile on his face as he drew his sword. The blunt hilt pressed deep against my abdomen and I felt the wind knocked out of my lungs. Bryan moved behind me and I found myself with the back of my head against his chest. I wound up in something like a head lock, but instead of his forearm the blade of his sword pressed up against my throat. He stood with his knee lifted to support my chest. If he removed his knee, I would have fallen to the ground against the razor-sharp blade. It would have decapitated me.

Scott put down his baseball bat.

"Now, my friend," Bryan said calmly. "You are going to calm down. OK?"

I was panting, but afraid to speak for fear that moving my jaw would place more pressure against the blade and my throat. Having a razor-sharp blade against one's neck probably inspires more terror than a gun pointed at one's head. I felt like I was bleeding, but I couldn't touch my neck because my hands were grasping Bryan's arms to support my weight and to keep my head on my shoulders. I wondered if any germs from the killing of the zombie could infect me from the sword's blade. I hoped whatever the antiseptic was that he used to clean it was effective.

"OK?" Bryan asked again as Scott pulled the handcuffs from my pocket.

"Please," I whispered.

I thought I was dead as the metal sliced across my throat. I fell to the ground at his feet. My hands went to my neck. It took me a moment to realize there was no blood. Bryan had turned the blade so that the dull back of it rather than the honed blade slid across my throat. Although I survived, to this day I can still feel the cold sensation and the terror of the heartless metal moving against the skin of my throat.

Scott yanked my arms behind my back and cuffed me. I offered no resistance. All my steam was spent on the two futile charges.

"Scott, cuff his hands in front so that he can catch himself if he falls." Bryan suggested.

"Won't he be able to fight us with his hands in front?" Scott asked with a sarcastic snort.

Bryan replied with a single huff like laugh.

"Yeah, I heard that," Scott laughed back.

With Bryan's sword's point indenting the skin of my back a few inches, I offered no physical resistance. However, I started screaming. "Help! Help!"

Bryan shook his head. "That will just attract more zombies."

"Then uncuff me so I can fight them, or I'll keep yelling."

Bryan just shook his head and after a moment said, "We'll need something more deadly than the zombies to scare him. Scott, give him the muffler."

"Sure, Bry." Scott drawled.

I curiously watched as Scott bent over and untied a fungus ridden boot. He removed his foot that was covered by an equally fungus covered sock. I could not even guess at the sock's original color. The manner in which he snickered started to scare me.

"What are you doing?" I asked as he slowly pulled the sock off of his foot. I coughed as I caught wind of the stench that over rode the scent of the rotter. "Geez! Have you ever changed socks in your life?"

"Why should I?" Scott laughed.

As he stepped forward, I blurted again, "What are you doing?"

He smiled and I saw a missing tooth. He held up the sock close to my face and answered my question, "Puttin' a sock in it, son. Now open up as we gag you." He looked at Bryan and said. "Tie that bandana around his mouth after I stick this in."

My jaw clamped shut as he attempted to stick the sock in my mouth.

I gagged and turned my head away from that atrocity, and begged through tight lips, "Please, I will keep quiet. Please. You have my word."

I dry heaved as the stinking thing touched my face. Scott gently brushed it across my cheek like a lover's caress as Bryan yanked my hair back, forcing my mouth to open.

Bryan laughed. "I think he learned his lesson."

"Oh," Scott whined as he held it before my open mouth for a moment.

"Thank you," I said breathlessly as Scott removed the offensive sock. "That would have been worse than being attacked by a zombie horde."

Bryan sadly agreed.

Scott's eyes crinkled in an avuncular manner. "I am starting to like you, kid. You're funny." he said with a laugh as he blindfolded me. I actually didn't mind because the blind fold was a cloth that was relatively clean.

Then a fear hit me. I worried that the blindfold was for a firing squad. I voiced that worry.

"The blindfold is so that you can't see the way to our camp," Bryan said.

They led me away. I stumbled a lot. I had enough trouble walking in the rocky Appalachian forest with sight. Without it, it was hell.

After I stumbled a few times, Scott said in a mock reverential tone of a cheesy martial art movie, "We take you to see Grand Masta, young grasshoppa."

"Who is that?" I asked.

"You are grasshoppa. That's who that." Scott said.

"No, I mean who is— "

Scott's laugh interrupted me.

Bryan said in his reasonable tone, "His name is Adam. He's basically our chief. He'll decide your fate. So, I suggest you kiss his ass when you meet him."

I trudged along blindfolded to meet my fate.

| 10 |

The light smell of wood smoke brought me out of my funk. In a world of darkness with the blindfold over my eyes and led with my hands securely bound, I found that my sense of smell won out as my favored sense in this moment. My ears had grown weary of Scott's incessant and utter nonsensical chatter, and I could barely hear that over the crunch of leaves beneath my feet. Oddly I could only rarely hear my captor's quiet footfalls.

On the other hand, I grew fond of Bryan's sensible character, but it annoyed me that he still had me handcuffed. That was unreasonable as well as the blindfold

There was a clean smell as we walked past a quickly flowing stream. The fallen dead leaves that we crunched through had an autumn smell.

I actually pondered for a moment what the scent of wood smoke must have stirred in me. I never really camped or did anything outdoorsy growing up, nor did I have a fireplace in any home and yet the smell of fire brought back a sort of nostalgia for a time that I never actually experienced personally. Maybe it was in my primal DNA, but it gave me a sense of coming home, despite the horrible circumstances.

I then heard the happy voices of children at play and I could actually sense a relaxation in my captors. Blindfolded, I couldn't visually pin exactly what signaled that they were relaxed, but maybe their stride shortened, the tugging on my leash wasn't as tight, but whatever it was, there wasn't the same sense of urgency, even though they paradoxically picked up the pace a small bit with the excitement of home.

I heard two children shout, "Daddy!"

I heard Bryan laugh and the leash went limp as I guess the children flung themselves into his arms causing him to forget about me.

I heard one of the kids ask, "Mommy, who is that stupid idiot?"

"Josiah! Don't talk like that!" A woman's voice scolded.

"But he's dressed like a clown and he was dumb enough to get captured and his hands cuffed. He must be a bad man," the child further accused

"No," said Bryan. "He's just confused."

"What's wrong with my clothes!?" I asked. I had bought some fashionable outdoors clothes before my excursion and hearing these backwoods rustics make fun of my clothes irritated me more for some reason. It soon dawned on me that my clothes were colorful and flashy, while theirs blended in with their surroundings. I had not even thought about that obvious consideration.

They ignored me and I could hear them explaining my capture. The tone of Scott's goofiness and then Bryan's dismissal of any danger that I presented also irritated my sense of pride. I would have preferred to have heard them tell a tale of exaggerated bravery and cunning. Yeah, I know, I went down easily, but I disliked being seen as harmless.

I finally yelled, "Can you take off the blindfold and let me film again now that we're home.

"What's this we?" asked Scott. "This may be our home, but you ain't home yet, son."

"Sorry about that, man," said Bryan as he removed my blind fold and then the handcuffs, "you can start filming if you get Adam's permission," he said.

I blinked a few times to adjust to the daylight and looked at my captors. I could feel the blood leave my face when I saw the woman. She held a baby. I looked at her two kids who happily ran around her. I looked at Bryan.

And then I looked back at her. Her eyes! It was her. It was indeed the family whose plight I had witnessed on the barroom's TV screen. I could not look away from her until Bryan said in a stern voice. "Is there something wrong with you?"

I realized that I was staring too long, too intensely into his wife's eyes.

"Anna?" Bryan addressed his wife. "Have you two met before?"

"No." she answered as she looked at me, unsure. Her eyes were curious, concerned. I was mesmerized as if meeting a celebrity.

I could now see suspicion and jealousy light Bryan's face. His eyes almost held the same intensity as when the drone filmed him in what I thought was his last stand just before he pulled the trigger on the gun.

"Is something wrong with you?" he asked. He pinned me with a glare and cocked his head, waiting for a response.

At the moment, I couldn't formulate the words to explain that I had spied on them through the drones. I was sure they held great hatred for the government who flew the drones. It would have marked me as an enemy to admit that I saw that even on national television. This wasn't a random guess. I had seen how he hated the drones with the anger in his eyes when he shot that one.

"No," I finally answered with a shake of my head. I unconsciously looked at her again which caused Bryan's jaw to clench and his eyes narrow.

I looked away as he grabbed my shoulder and pushed me ahead. "Get going," he ordered. All of his reasonableness vanished.

Someone shouted, "Hey, go easy on him. We are not savages up here." I later learned that the guy who defended me was named Tomas.

Bryan ignored him.

I stumbled with the push, and righted myself. As I stood, my eyes went to the hills above and I did a double take. I swore I saw an actual skeleton clothed in a hooded cloak standing, staring, grinning back at me. With a terror that I had never felt before, I looked back up and indeed it was a skeleton face on a man-like creature dressed in black paramilitary fatigues under a black cloak, but it looked like he was maybe wearing a skeletal mask of some sort. The skeleton man stared at me for a moment and then with a muscular lunge of his huge body, he disappeared behind a boulder. My absolute terror was replaced by a fear. The skeleton man appeared like it wanted to be seen by me. Was he a member of the tribe or something entirely different?

As I stood pondering, I received a vicious shove from behind and went sprawling on the ground.

"Move," Bryan ordered.

"Hey," Tomas scolded again, and again Bryan ignored him.

"Who was that?" I asked.

"Tomas?" Bryan asked.

"No, the..." I didn't know how to say it.

"Who was what?" Bryan demanded.

"The skeleton man on the hill," I finally stated.

"Quit your crazy talk and get up," Bryan ordered. However, he nervously looked over the surrounding mountains. I could tell that he knew there were strange things about.

I stood up and avoided looking at Bryan or his family, especially his wife and looked ahead to the village as we crested a rise in the trail. As we crossed over the ridgeline, I finally saw the structures where they lived.

My heart sank.

Based on the Robin Hood and his Merry Men fantasy, I was hoping to see Hobbit style homes or tree houses. Instead, I saw a filthy squatter's camp. All the shelters were teepees, each made with two or more threadbare tarps of mismatched colors. Light smoke wafted from the tops of a few of them. Chickens, cats, dogs, and a few goats walked among the people. The inhabitants were thin, but physically fit. They walked erect, with a pride that I wasn't expecting in such squalor.

I noted that I instinctively braced for the stench of urine and feces that I had encountered at refugee camps during my brief time as a journalist in the Mideast and Central America. However, it was absent. I later learned that they were very particular about burying any waste to prevent disease and attract undesirables: animals, people, and those who used to be people. Hygiene was so enforced that people could drink from the small stream that meandered through the camp. Of course, they drank upstream because they couldn't train the livestock to bury its waste. I found out that leaving anything organic to rot on the ground was treated with extreme punishment.

I also learned that they regularly moved camps to follow game and to avoid other tribes from detecting them from the trails that became ingrained in the hills from their repetitive travels.

Men, women, and children moved about at ease but with a sense of purpose. They appeared confident in their security, but they had a peaceful alertness as they did their chores. They smoked meats, scraped hides, or worked with various gadgets that were a mix of modern and primitive ingenuity, most of which the purpose escaped me at that time. The gadgets seemed to be for daily living rather than anything arcane. Even the dogs, chickens, goats and a few other animals meandered about on their own missions as well.

In the center of the camp by the communal fire, I saw one man gracefully practice some martial forms with a Japanese sword. I took it for a dull practice blade because he swung it and caught the blade under his arm pit where the big brachial artery was, but after a few moves, I saw him cleanly slice through a stout staff. He made eye contact with me, nodded, and I looked away. I later learned that he went by the name Critter. He looked slightly younger than Bryan, maybe late twenties or early thirties.

As I turned away from Critter, I looked straight into the reflective glasses of an old man. There was nothing in his stature or muscular frame that was spectacular or made him stand out. However, there was something in the way he stood, maybe an assuredness in the face or posture, it wasn't anger or a challenge but rather supreme confidence from him that made me look down. I instinctively knew that he was Adam or as Scott put it sarcastically, the Grand Masta.

He chuckled as if at some cosmic irony, "What the heck did you two drag back to my porch," he asked Scott and Bryan.

"You must be Adam." I said extending my hand.

He shook it but kept any feelings off of his face.

Scott instantly chimed up, "We brought you slick, here. He scared away some potential dinner, but he claims he'll make us famous. He must have heard how legendary my pecker is all the way back from where he's from."

The old man made no reaction to Scott's attempt at humor. "Did you see anything else?"

"Just a wuh-wuh," Bryan said with no humor.

"What's a wah-wah?" Adam asked.

Scott shrugged and replied, "Apparently it's what them there people up in New York call the zombies. He seemed incapable of saying anything else in the zombie's presence. They must worship zombies as much as they worship me."

"I see." The old man cracked a grin and shook his head. "Follow protocol. Then we'll have a chat."

"You got it. Come on," Bryan said. He was back to his mellow nature.

I followed him to one of the tarp teepees. Bryan rapped a knuckle against the taut plastic which resounded like a drum and a sweet feminine voice from inside the tent replied. "Yes?"

"Hey, Shelley. Adam wants to interview a lost boy," Bryan announced.

"Come in," she said invitingly.

Bryan threw a tarp aside forming a doorway and ushered me inside. I entered. It took my eyes a moment to adjust. Shelly was a thin, older woman with an elegance that I could see despite the rustic clothing. She stood up from a cross legged position without using her hands for assistance and extended one towards me.

I shook it and she directed me to have a seat, which I did. Somehow, she seemed to have as much power in her gentle suggestions as Don had in his harsh words and violence.

"You may go," she said to Bryan.

"Are you sure?" he asked.

"I am sure," Shelley replied.

A small fire in the center of the tent heated a small pot. She offered me a cup of tea from the pot. I gratefully accepted and felt it slip warmth into my hands, which were cold from the dreary winter day. I sipped the tea. It was delicious. I could detect mint and a few pleasant tastes that I couldn't pinpoint.

"I love this. Where did you get this tea?" I asked.

"The convenience store down the creek," she said with such grace that I didn't hear the obvious sarcasm.

"Where?" I asked with genuine curiosity.

"The forest plants are my convenience store these days," she said with a distant look through the opaque tarp.

"I taste mint." I said.

She smiled, "I usually avoid mints in my tea in winter because of their cooling effect on the body, but today I thought catnip would be appropriate."

"Meow," I replied in a deadpan voice.

She laughed like a songbird chirping. Although I think that her laugh at my poor attempt at humor was strictly polite.

We talked for twenty minutes. I relaxed in her presence. Maybe it was one of the herbs in the tea, but I divulged more info than I meant to when I replayed the conversation later that night. It was mostly personal stuff rather than my mission.

A sharp knock on the taut plastic and then the rustle of the entrance tarp thrown aside startled me. Adam, Bryan, Scott and Critter walked inside the confines of the small tent. I was intimidated as the men stood over me, slightly stooped from the low ceiling.

I started to stand.

"Stay seated," Bryan ordered with a hand on my shoulder.

Scott wordlessly dropped my backpack with my equipment by my side.

"I think he's OK." Shelley said.

"I gathered that," said Adam. He looked at me and said. "You may not leave the perimeter of the main campfire, and at night, you must remain in the tent we provide."

"I have a tent that I can sleep in." I really didn't want to sleep on a dirt floor in one of those hovels.

"No. Your tent is a good one. We will save it to use for when we must travel in a hurry," Bryan explained as if the tent belonged to him. At the moment, I didn't protest.

Adam said, "I am confident you will be allowed to join our tribe, but first we must get a consensus."

"I thought it was your decision," I said as I pulled out my video camera.

Adam laughed with grandfatherly kindness and said, "You flatter me with power that I do not wield. I simply provide a possible direction for this herd of cats."

I found that this was a simplification. I later learned that they had a system of law that was brutally enforced. However, any tribe member was free to avoid punishment and leave in exile. Very few chose to leave in this mad world.

"May I start filming?" I asked, neglecting to tell him that I had been filming the whole time with the camera vest and cap that Tommy had provided me. However, I wanted to film with my actual camera for a more professional looking documentary.

"Yes, you may," Adam replied.

I heard a quiet exhale from Bryan and could see he wasn't happy.

Adam continued, "However, Bryan will review anything you film. I am sure you understand that our very lives depend on certain secrets."

I was really hoping to interview Bryan and find out how he survived the horde after he shot down the drone, but he turned and left through the flap without a word.

I turned to Adam and asked, "Could I interview you, with the camera rolling?"

"Sorry, but I am busy. However, we'll need you to stand up and take off your clothes." Adam said as if such a demand was perfectly normal.

"What?" I asked in shock.

Adam explained, "Nothing perverted, but we must check you for bites. It's our protocol. Too many times, seemingly healthy people have come to reside with us and turned into zombies when we least expected it. You may keep your underwear on."

I complied and he and Shelley looked me over. She was a type of healer, I realized, specializing in herbalism.

"Hold still," said Adam, "and don't worry, I am a doctor."

I learned he was truthful, although he was a veterinarian.

The old man pulled on my waist band and looked down the front and back of my underwear quickly with stern professionalism. He said, "I apologize, but it's a necessity. He's safe," Adam announced. Then he said, "If you would excuse me."

Adam left without waiting for anyone to excuse him.

"You can point the camera at me. I gots lots to tell. I am the Earl of that Kardashian Kingdom you talked about."

Not wanting to hear anything more from Scott, I said politely, "I heard a lot from you on our hike over here. I'd like to meet someone else. I've heard enough about your pecker."

The people smiled, and even Scott laughed.

Critter said, "Yep, we've all heard enough. He needs new material."

I could tell that Critter didn't want to get interviewed, but I really didn't want to spend another five minutes with the man who attempted to stick his rancid sock in my mouth.

"How about you, sir?"

"I guess," he answered morosely. "Names Christopher but— "

"—But people call you Critter. I heard others call you that." I retorted with an edge of sarcasm. I didn't mean that, but having spent the last twenty-four hours feeling totally humiliated, returning to my natural line of work gave me a sense of overconfidence that I longed to re-establish.

He gave me an irritated look and left the tent. "Forget it," he muttered.

"Thanks for the tea, Shelley." I called over my shoulder.

She nodded graciously and I followed Critter.

I stepped outside and caught Anna's eye, but quickly looked away so as not to anger Bryan. In the brief eye contact I could tell that I had intrigued her in some way. There was softness in the way she looked at me.

I noticed Critter avoided her as well.

I ran to catch him as I got my camera rolling and ready. He walked to the main campfire. "Hey, man, I'm sorry," I apologized. I kept the video camera rolling but kept it at my side so he could see that my face was serious.

"Don't sweat it. I'm on edge. When Bryan came home with his family…"

"Are you guys enemies?" I prompted, but worried that I was pushing my curious questioning too far, too fast.

"Oh no, no. He's like a brother to me, but I've searched everywhere for my wife and kids. It's been over a year. I've had to assume they're dead. Bryan got a long shot lead and brought his family back last week. I am happy for him, but seeing his happiness only reminds me of my lack of happiness. It's rekindled a false hope that I had gotten over, or I had gotten over at one time."

I nodded, surprised at his bluntness, and looked at Bryan who was involved in a heated argument with his wife. I also noted in the forty or fifty some people of the tribe, most of the inhabitants were men. Men at their horniest age range. I could guess at such dynamics in a violent world.

I wanted to ask about Bryan's fight that I saw from the drone footage, but I realized I needed to change the subject fast.

"Who are you guys?" I asked.

"We've acquired the name Mountain Warriors. Most of us are martial artists, survival teachers or students. We were doing a weeklong seminar, called Mountain Warriors, in these mountains when it all went down. Bryan came up with that name actually. He got us all together originally. Well, him and Adam."

"Are there others, other groups of survivors in the area?"

He made a sour face and shrugged. "There are some. The nearest are the Low Boys. They live at the base of our mountain. Resources are scarce. Half the times we trade with them, the other times we fight them. Sometimes we join forces."

He saw the curious look on my face.

"We abide by an unwritten code that changes often. There is an odd fellowship of survivors against the undead, even if your fellow survivor is an enemy on occasion."

"Undead? You mean zombies?" I asked.

He shook his head ruefully. "Them and also I've heard rumors of vampires. They are basically zombies with intelligence. We've found people with blood sucked from their arteries and have seen some strange, repellant people from a distance."

I mentioned the skeleton man, "I saw a man up the mountain, spying on us. It looked like he wore a skeleton's mask. Is he one of them?"

"You probably saw The Specter." Critter mused.

The name sent a shiver down my spine. The use of the word "specter" seemed to stir up every superstitious dread that

I had buried since childhood. The casual use of that word as if such a horror was now a normal occurrence was almost too much. He saw the fear in my eyes and shrugged dismissively.

"Don't sweat it. He's some power hungry..." he left it hanging.

I was thoroughly intrigued, "A power hungry what? Man? Vampire? Thing?"

"I don't know. He's been sighted with the Low Boys recently." He looked at me with new curiosity. "You're from outside. What causes this, undeadness? Bacteria, virus, poison? Are they, the scientists, are they nearing a cure or vaccination? How was it started? A government test gone wrong?"

I shrugged. "I thought it was spread by getting bit?"

He looked at me angrily, "That's comic book crap! You, the ones outside this death zone, are the ones who have the scientists, the laboratories, the time to study this stuff! We only have the opportunity to eke out enough to barely survive. Look how thin we all are. To be honest, getting bitten is one way to get it, but we're still unsure how contagious it is. We're unsure if some of us have an immunity. That would be nice to know, but I'm not going to test it out. I stay away from those freaks, and wash like a germaphobe if one even just walks by or if I smell one."

"I really don't know anything about it. There is a media blackout. That's why I decided to investigate," I explained.

He nodded and seemed somewhat satisfied. "Yeah, I imagine they keep everyone in the dark. All those weirdo conspiracy theorists turned out to be onto the truth." His mood suddenly turned dark as if memories of everything he had lost were suddenly in his vision. His fists seemed to tense at those who were behind this, yet too far from his rage, far from his sword and guns of vengeance for him to be able to do anything about it.

I changed the subject again before he could get too dark. "What's your specialty? I mean are you an instructor or student?"

He replied, "At this point, everyone is both, including you if you want to survive. Teach what you know, learn what you can."

"So, what are your skills? I saw your work with the sword, the kata, I believe it's called. It was both graceful and deadly," I said. It wasn't mere flattery. His skill and grace did impress me.

"Thanks. At this point everyone needs to know swordplay, but back in the day, I taught trapping critters for food and essentials. Hence my nickname. I also taught knife throwing."

"That's cool. Do you have a throwing knife here?" I asked.

"I have more than 'a' throwing knife," he laughed. His face changed with the change of subject. His eyes were bright with youthful excitement. "Hey, punch me," he requested with an odd anticipation.

He looked very confident. I figured that he'd tighten his abs and could take it, so I cocked my fist back to give a good punch to his gut.

"No," he scolded lightheartedly. I noticed that as we spoke of fighting his morose attitude lessened and disappeared completely. I realized that this guy really liked fighting or at least the fighting arts.

"What?" I asked.

"Make it a good punch. No love pats." He said smiling as he patted his belly. Oddly, his belly wasn't tensed. It was relaxed and even extended slightly as if daring or even inviting me.

I smiled and wound my fist back even farther and let it go at his belly.

"Ouch!" I yelled as my fist hit a solid object.

He laughed and withdrew two twelve-inch throwing blades from sheaths on the belly of his jacket. He tossed one right after another at the post fifteen feet away. Both stuck with a solid thunking sound.

I then noticed the different sheaths distributed over his body in areas that an opponent would slash with a sword or punch with a fist. Many of the sheaths had stitched up lacerations showing that he had put them to good use where swords had gashed them. Critter held his arm toward me so I could pat the outside of his sleeve. I could feel knives in the places where he could use his arm to block a blow or use to strike back.

"Cool idea. I've never seen armor that could be weaponized like that," I said.

Critter smacked some of his armor and said, "An old Filipino trick I learned. I never thought that I would use it in real life until it all went down."

I then walked to the post and with some effort withdrew the knives from deep in the wood. I studied the damage the blades made to the wood, "Dang. These are a few inches deep."

"Don't be too impressed. A bullet from a gun would have blown a hole straight through and kept on going."

"Don't bring a gun to a knife fight, huh?" I said trying to sound tough, but it didn't feel natural off of my lips. I felt like I was trying too hard to sound tough. These people here were just simply tough. There was no façade with them.

"Something like that," he answered. "Although we do try to stick with blades for safety."

Critter started looking morose again, so I tried to steer the conversation back to his interest.

I pointed to the rifle slung across his back and the handgun on his hip. "I notice everyone that I've met carries a gun or two like it's fashionable, but everyone is a sword and knife freak as well. Why is that?" Don had explained already, but I was curious if he had told me the truth.

Critter spat at the fire and said, "Those zombies respond to noises. They prefer to stick to flat ground, like roads or occasionally trails. That's why we prefer the high country. However, they will follow a sound. If a gun is fired, it's like they forget everything and follow that. It's uncanny. You'll see them show up at a place two, even three, days after a gun has been fired. Hordes of those bastards."

"Yeah," I agreed. "On the helicopter ride I saw a whole bunch of them in a valley nearby. Probably thousands." I said this hoping it would be great intelligence for them and maybe they'd accept me. However, I was disappointed. They already knew about the horde.

"Yeah, that's why we're being extra quiet. We're probably going to leave within a week. Too much risk staying here. One of us might do something stupid or a lone lost hunter might shoot nearby and we'll be up to our eyeballs in those things. Heck, the zombies might just get a wild hair and show up here if they catch a strong whiff of us. You never know with these damn things." Again, his mood turned dark. I felt like he was fantasizing about strangling those on the outside who he blamed for all of this, probably my uncle.

Critter liked talking about firearms, knives and survival skills, so I changed the subject back, "Are there a lot of firearms in camp?"

Critter started to open his mouth, but closed it as Bryan arrived and said sharply. "He doesn't need to know that." Bryan turned to me and asked, "Why are you asking such questions? Are you spying for someone?"

"I am a journalist and guns and other weaponry seems to be something that interests you guys. So, I asked." I spoke honestly.

Bryan replied back, "It's not some interest or hobby. It's a means for survival, and that is not information that we want to get out. It's time for you to go to your tent for the night, spy."

Critter said, "Bry, it's O.K."

"No, it's not, O.K. I don't like him pumping us for info. We really have no idea who he is, what he wants or more importantly, who he works for. He's the Governor's nephew!"

"Bry, I was going to teach him to throw a knife. Adam told us that he could--" Critter began.

However, I was getting tired of everybody speaking for me. I planted my feet and told Bryan, "Adam gave me permission to do my job as a journalist, and I will hold him and you to that. Besides it isn't even dark yet."

Bryan stepped up to me. His eyes were chips of ice. There was no humanity in them. Something had changed. I felt more fear of him than I had when facing Don.

He growled, "Adam is busy, and so I'm changing things. Whatever happens to our tribe because of you will rest on my shoulders because I brought you here. Besides, we have weapons laying about, and I wouldn't want you to hurt yourself. So, you will listen to me."

I noticed his hand was on his sword so I responded diplomatically, "Alright. I will do as you say, but I want to speak to Adam and anyone else who decides my fate as soon as possible."

"Very well. For now, you will wait in your tent. Any attempted escape will result in immediate execution." He walked away and without looking at me said, "Follow me."

I obeyed. I had no choice.

| 11 |

I sat alone in the tent with an odd mix of boredom, restlessness, and fear. It was driving me nuts entrusting my future into the hands of people who now scared the crap out of me, especially in a land where I had no chance at survival on my own. Even if these people fully accepted me, I was still literally at their mercy. I would have to rely on them to feed, shelter and protect me. I was tired of my fate resting in the hands of others. I wanted to act. I wanted to be in charge of my own destiny. That urge was almost overpowering. I decided I had to learn every method of fighting that they knew, until my eyes could go as icy as Bryan's when he was provoked.

It also infuriated me that they would see the need to lock me in the tent. It wasn't like I had any desire to attempt escape. In fact, they probably would have loved it if I had just walked off. My disappearance was more food for the bellies of Bryan's kids. What stung worse was that Bryan claimed I was locked up for my own safety, so that I didn't hurt myself with their weapons. Their kids played with swords and around guns. The people of the tribe had no respect for me at all.

It was ridiculous. They just didn't trust me. They truly thought of me as a spy, but what the hell would someone want from this stranded bunch of penniless survivors? It was idiotic paranoia.

Also, in this inactivity, I was acutely aware of every physical insult that I suffered. From my facial injury when I bashed into the tree, to my ass where Don literally kicked it, there was an icky feeling on my throat where I rested on Bryan's blade, to the middle knuckle of my right fist where I punched Critter's throwing knife. Also, it seemed that every joint was tortured from my running, hiking, crawling, scrambling and of course falling and sliding into trees. An oppressive exhaustion was mixed with all that but as I said, I was restless as hell too.

On top of that were my psychological insults. I forced myself not to cry. I looked like a fool in front of Tommy, Don, and to these strangers. I had totally misdiagnosed myself. It was not that I lacked success in my life. It was that I accepted failure and expected to walk away from it. It was my weakness. I was no man at all. I gave up too often. I wept when I should have acted. If action was not an option at this time, I should plan for when action was appropriate.

It was in this moment I made a solemn vow, never to be weak again. I may renege on my sobriety and drink again. I might be defeated. I might even die in the next hour, but, I solemnly vowed, I would never quit again, cry, or show any weakness. Win or failure didn't so much matter. I would launch on any endeavor to strengthen my body, mind, and soul.

For the first time in my life, I meant something. I firmly punched my fist into the dirt of the tent's floor and felt the pain shoot up from my knuckle. I forced myself not to overreact. I told myself that the pain was self-inflicted and would pass, as I rubbed the knuckle. That somewhat worked at relieving the pain.

Alone with my thoughts, my mind drifted away from my current issues. I replayed the moment that Bryan subjugated me and held his blade against my throat. He wasn't even forced to use effort to subdue me. It was all a joke to him. I was a joke to him. I wanted that bastard to take me seriously. I wanted him to hold me in the same respect that I held him when I witnessed his fighting spirit from the drone footage. I wanted to own that fighting spirit in my own heart. I wanted it to blaze through my own eyes. I wanted others to see that strength in me.

I was picturing the different maneuvers that I could have used not just to avoid that painful and humiliating sword choke, but how I could have reversed it and pinned Bryan, or even better, literally knocked that smug ass look off of his face. I wanted a rematch!

I then fantasized about using some moves from a myriad of cheesy kung fu movies on Bryan. I didn't mind that the moves either would not work or that I would mess them up when faced with the stress of reality. I purposely made his butt-kicking melodramatic, silly, and humorous, just to relieve the tension that had built in my mind.

It was at this moment that I was scared out of my fantasy by a shuffling noise from a corner of my tent. I looked over expecting to see some skeletal beast slipping under the tent, but instead it was a folded piece of paper that someone had slid through the small space between the dirt floor and the tarp wall.

I picked it up and unfolded it with both curiosity and apprehension. I flicked on my headlamp and read the scrawl. It was from Anna.

Dearest Eric,

Please help me escape the torment that is my husband, Bryan. I can see in your eyes that you are a good man and have feelings for me. I know a place of safety where we will both be protected from that monster. I undid the latch on the tent. Meet me behind your tent immediately if you agree to escape with me. Please be quiet as you move, but be quick. Time is of the essence.

Love,

Anna

My first reaction was that she must have written it in great distress because it was choppy handwriting for a woman.

I heard someone undoing the rope on the outside of my tent. I heard the rope lightly slide against the tarp to the ground, and I heard soft footsteps retreating around to the back of my tent. The footsteps stopped where she waited.

A sense of urgency that I had never felt before kicked in. I quickly folded the note, placed it in my pocket. I impulsively moved towards the entrance flap quickly and quietly. I pushed aside the tarp and stepped outside. I looked around but the coast was clear. I instinctively smelled the air for the person who was just there, but I could only smell the forest and wood smoke. I tiptoed around the crude shelter of my prison. I tripped over a guide rope and landed with a thud. I cursed sharply and then abruptly shut my mouth.

Inwardly, I cursed myself some more for my outburst. I looked around but no one in the nighttime camp seemed curious about my release of expletives. I quickly jumped to my feet and ran around the corner.

I slammed on the brakes, digging my heels in as I saw the flash of a steel blade. The sword tip pushed deep against my belly. The point was a milligram of pressure away from shredding my clothes and penetrating my abdomen.

I looked up from the blade into Bryan's fierce eyes. "Running off with my wife? You son of a bitch!"

| 12 |

I returned his glare. "What did you do to her?"

"So, you admit it. You were going to run off with her." Bryan said. He smiled victoriously, but his eyes held a homicidal fury.

"I'm rescuing her, you brute!" I was not scared at all. The note inspired a bit of chivalry in me that I wasn't previously aware of as well as I was powered by the sincerity of my latest vow. If I were to die now, I would be damned before I got a tear in my eye.

"You? You think you could rescue her?" he scoffed.

I didn't rise to his taunt. "She said you were tormenting her," I glared at him.

"She didn't write that," he said with a cruel smile.

I was about to ask who, but I looked into his smug eyes and could tell it was he who set me up as a fool.

"For what purpose?" now I was seething with a rage I had never felt before.

"I saw the way you were looking at her," he accused.

"You jackass!" I exclaimed. "I was staring at her because I've seen you all before! I just didn't believe it in the moment."

He scoffed and I felt the slightest extra pressure on my belly. I was mere seconds and milligrams of pressure from death.

Before he could literally spill my guts, I told him how I saw the plight of his family from the drone footage. I explained that I was looking at her because I had just realized that he and his family had survived the zombie attack, and meeting them was like meeting a celebrity. It was seeing his family's determination to live that inspired me to leave my life for this hell hole in the first place.

He looked at me skeptically. The sword point was still indenting my belly by a few inches and Bryan seemed literally dead set to puncture me. "If I so fascinated you, then why were you looking to run off with my wife."

A new wave of fury hit me and my belly actually pushed slightly back against the point of his blade as I leaned in toward him. He even released some of the pressure so as not to let me kill myself.

I raged, "Because in the letter-- She claimed that you were tormenting her! I didn't know you would be so dishonest! You forged a letter to play me a fool! To play on my chivalry!" Chivalry was a corny word but it suddenly and oddly had a true meaning.

He relaxed some more on the pressure of the sword and laughed, "And you would be willing to cross swords with me to save a damsel in distress? A damsel, I might add, who could easily kick your ass."

I just glared at him.

He sobered and asked. "Enough crap. What is your real purpose here?"

"I wanted to hear the truth." I said looking him full in the eyes.

The pressure of his sword tip lessened a little more.

Bryan blinked a few times as he considered my words. He raised both eyebrows and then arched just one as he seemed to study my soul. He nodded his head as if he had discovered something about me. He addressed me so formally that at first, I wasn't sure if it was true honor or sarcasm. "So, you would die for the truth? On the surface it sounds foolish, but that is a rare virtue. Honorable indeed." He bowed with an almost Japanese formality, he then withdrew the katana's tip from my belly and resheathed it with a reverential spinning flourish of the weapon. He turned his back on me and walked towards the communal campfire.

I stood there, still not sure of anything.

He stopped and looked back at me. "Come with me. If you would like to hear the truth."

***

I followed him to the campfire. He offered me a cigarette. I didn't smoke anymore, but I gratefully accepted. I had noticed in the past that sharing a substance of any sort often made conversation easier.

Bryan smiled lazily. "I never smoked in the past. After the whole ordeal went down, I experimented with nicotine because it wasn't readily available like it had been. It gives me a nice head buzz. Cigars are really nice in the summer because they keep mosquitoes away."

We lit up and both enjoyed a few puffs. There's something that feels both primal and home like about a campfire. I watched the smoke rise and disappear into the darkness as if watching souls ascend to their heavenly home. The rest of the camp was quiet. With the darkness free of electronic light, people went to sleep as naturally as a babe at his mother's bosom. I again thought of how men were like birds, put to sleep with the cover of darkness.

"You're free to wander," Bryan said. "I trust you now. I apologize for my earlier deception, with the fake letter from my wife."

"Why do you suddenly trust me now?" I asked. Although I was grateful for the sudden change of attitude, it filled me with suspicion. "Was it something I said?"

"No. It's a gut instinct. The sincerity in your eyes, the way you pressed back against the point of the blade. I tend to believe what a man does, rather than what he says."

I nodded and took a drag. We both contemplated the mingling and diverging and reconverging smoke streams.

He added after a pause in our conversation, "This world is crazy. I guess it always has been. It's just easier to see now. An apocalypse makes things more honest. Can you understand how you appear to us? Especially when you were interested in our firearms. We have enemies who have literally killed members of our group to discover such secrets."

I just nodded. For the moment I savored the relief from the harsh glare of suspicion.

"So, what would you like to know?" He asked.

I shrugged. I was suddenly speechless.

He laughed, "You go through hell just to ask questions and then you don't have any questions when given the opportunity?"

"It's all a jumble of a thousand questions." It was odd how the ordeal had seemed to wipe my mind clean when given this sudden relief.

Bryan said, "It reminds me of when I was a kid. I was at this park and I saw thousands of silvery minnows swimming in a pool under a water fountain. I tried catching a minnow by reaching into the mass, but they all kept slipping away. Another boy kept catching them easily and then releasing them one right after another. He was no quicker than me. I asked him how he did it, and he said with the assuredness of a science nerd, 'you're focusing on the whole mass of minnows. I only focus on one at a time.' That worked. I started catching them as quickly as he was. Pick only one question at a time. Get it?"

"I had the main question answered by seeing you and your family alive." I said. I then asked the next obvious question, "What happened to that bandit?"

"What bandit?" he asked.

"You know, that group that tried to rob you or something. You killed three men and then faced off with that big bald dude with the braided beard."

"Oh, you mean Craig," Bryan laughed as if I mentioned a lifelong friend. "He's a tough guy. He taught Krav Maga before it all went down."

"What's that? Some exotic cuisine?" I joked.

"A very hard-nosed martial art that was taught to Israeli commandos."

"Whoa." I replied. "I thought he would give you a run for your money, but then you guys joined forces against that horde."

"He's still around. Craig was an old school mate of mine. In the neighborhood, as kids, we'd played football in the morning, fight in the afternoon, and then be friends again long enough to have another football game before our mothers called us in for the night."

"You sound like you still like him?"

"It was nothing personal," he said, shrugging a threat to his life off like rain gathered in a pocket of a tarp shelter.

"You seem rather casual about a potential blood feud," I said, quite taken aback by his calm demeanor.

"Tempers can flare in a zombie apocalypse," he replied with irony in his tone at saying "zombie apocalypse." "Resources are limited. In another life we'd still be friends, good friends. Hell, we may still be friends, but I won't hesitate to kill him if need be. It's sad. Our kids used to play together.

Hell, we half-jokingly pledged that his daughter would marry my oldest boy."

Where is he? Craig?" I asked.

"He runs a group down the hill."

"Oh, the Low Boys?"

He looked at me with suspicion welling up again. This was getting annoying.

I explained, "Critter said they were your main rivals." I paused then asked, "So loyalty to the living overrides your rivalry for resources."

He nodded. "It would be easy to channel a zombie herd up their cove to his town and wipe out the Low Boys, but we have an unwritten law against that. I would never doom a person to the cursed life of the undead, no matter what he did to me. I hope he feels the same way. To me and most people, turning into a zombie is worse than death."

"Yeah, Critter said you guys have a lot of unwritten codes like avoiding using guns in favor of blades or bats."

We try not to use weapons at all on other humans. If we can settle something with a verbal argument or a fist fight and let each other walk away, that's better. We have a loose 'eye for an eye' rule also," he said. "Once I cross blades, it's usually a fight to the death, but Craig caught me at a rough time."

"What was that," I asked when Bryan hesitated.

"I had just found my family after we'd been separated for over a year. My wife and I went through hell finding each other and escaping back into the mountains. Losing my wife and kids again at that point wasn't an option after what I went through to find and retrieve them. Hell, I kind of regret drawing on Craig, but they pushed it. You know, I might even head down there to the Low Boy's village in a couple days to trade some extra honey or mead that we have and see if we're still O.K. We're not savages after all."

I looked away so that he would not see my temporary perplexion on my face. Bryan was casually writing off an attack on, not just his life, but the life of his family, and I doubted that Craig would dismiss the confrontation with equal flippancy. Bryan claimed not to be a savage, yet I had witnessed him dish out violent and forceful savagery.

I looked over as his eyes turned up toward the distant stars with equally distant pondering or longing for something intangible. It was then that I solved the Bryan conundrum. What had perplexed me was that he spoke in a soft mellow voice and used words and grammar that varied from a movie land version of an ancient Kung Fu master to even that of a Shakespearean actor. My guess, and it later proved correct, was that he had unintentionally modeled his speech to that of what he considered to be a noble warrior. He wished to elevate himself and loved ones from the obvious brutal state of existence through his speech and mannerisms. Although at times the reality of the situation demanded barbaric action for the survival of the ones that he loved. It was similar to me unconsciously adopting the accents of the different locations that I had traveled.

As much as I wanted to ask about this subject, I knew from my experience from past interviews that the worst thing to do is to make a psychological assumption about the interviewee. They tend to offer vociferous denials. Instead I asked about Scott, his seemingly polar opposite.

"I notice that Scott seems to butcher the English language at times, but other times he is almost well spoken."

Bryan laughed. "That's good observation. There is a lot more to him than meets the eyes."

Bryan was about to leave it at that so I prompted, "But you can say that about everybody you'll ever meet."

"Such as yourself," he said and then sighed, "Yeah well, his Father actually owned a paper mill over in Tennessee. His family was quite rich in a very poor town. I feel that he tries to pretend that he isn't well-bred to fit in. I've met his brother. By their language, you'd never guess they were from the same household."

I nodded and said, "but sometimes he seems to go beyond the normal colloquialisms."

Bryan chuckled and lazily tossed a small twig into the fire sending a few sparks into the night sky. He explained, "I think he tries to get under my skin. If he plays on a joke, he tends to overplay it to an atrocious degree. I am usually pretty particular about my own language."

I shrugged innocently.

He didn't buy it, "Surely, if you have noticed Scott's lingo, you are well aware of my manner of speech, which Anna calls 'stiltedly formal,' especially after this all went down."

I conceded a nod.

"Any other questions?" he asked.

I thought for a moment and then the whir of a drone caught my attention.

"Why did you shoot out the drone and how did you survive that mass attack that I watched? This is the question that's been intriguing me the most," I admitted.

He cast his eyes to the direction of the whine of a drone's rotors somewhere in the dark. I could see fierce resentment in his eyes for those machines and what and who they represented. I, on the other hand, nervously thought of Don's warning about them packing enough explosives to level a house.

Bryan said, "I'd rather not answer that question. We need some secrets from them."

"Dude, I'm stuck out here. I'm one of you guys now, an outcast. Anything you say is between us."

He looked away from the drone and pinned me with a flash of that same resentment. "You don't have a hidden camera, do you? You're not recording this, are you?"

I didn't mean to lie, but I still feared him. I quickly denied it without having a chance to process his question. "Of course not," I blurted. I would come to regret this lie, but in the meantime, I changed the subject. "Drones can't pick up sounds," I reassured him.

"Still, I would rather not say, and I hope you don't find out why I shot the drone."

"Why is that?" I asked.

"Because we'll be in a similar perilous moment and I don't think you will survive," he said.

The bluntness of his statement caught me off guard. I just stared at him as he stood up from the ground where he had sat.

"You're free to move about, but not free to do something stupid, but I recommend that you get some sleep. You will need it. Tomorrow morning will be very busy for you. Good night."

"What's going on tomorrow?" I asked his back as he walked away. He either didn't hear or he ignored me. "Good night," I muttered back.

***

Unbeknownst to me at the time and ten miles away in the valley below, Craig, the leader of the Low Boys stood alone in the darkened forest. He was a strong, broad man. He waited for someone. He cast an angry glance at the ubiquitous drone hovering above his head. He couldn't see it in the darkness, but he could hear the mini rotors whining like a persistent child.

"Those things annoy the hell out of you, don't they?" said an inhumanly low-pitched voice as if from the grave.

Craig casually turned as if he had been expecting the visitor from the deep forest. A tall man stepped forward. His massive muscular physique rippled beneath the paramilitary black clothes and equally black cloak. Only piercing dark eyes could be seen behind the skull faced masked that was uncannily realistic.

Craig ignored the question. The visitor knew the answer.

Craig disliked the meetings with the mysterious Specter. The deep gravelly voice wasn't a normal human voice. Craig didn't know if it was purposely modified with the intent of intimidating or to camouflage his identity like the mask. Rumors ricocheted like bullets through his town that the voice was his natural voice and that the strange mask and voice were due to a horrific injury, either that or mutations from the zombie virus. As imposing as the mask was, people feared that the malformed features that lurked beneath the mask were even more evil.

"Hey Specter. What's the word?" Craig asked, getting straight to business. The sooner the business was done with this creature the better.

The Specter's eyes crinkled in a smile. "The vampires are on the move. I suggest making a deal with them before the Mountain Warriors do."

"We will get to that later. Speaking of the Mountain Posers?" Craig let his words hang.

"Your mistake has benefited us. Our infiltrator is in place. That clown named Eric. He's the adopted son of the Governor Hildebrande," The Specter's voice grated.

"We looked for him, Specter," Craig pleaded.

"You fools let the Mountain Warriors get him!" The Specter shouted like a ferocious bark from a savage dog, "but it will still work for us."

"We got there as soon as the chopper left," Craig insisted almost in a plea.

"Not soon enough, obviously."

"Why didn't you guys wait for us?"

"The pilots can't know of our contact," The Specter shouted. The skeletal man feared nothing in the night and didn't worry about his loud voice.

"Didn't the pilots check for anyone else in the area?"

"Quit asking questions as if you are in charge. However, I think it will work out fine for now. The fool doesn't realize we can hear and see everything he records. He thinks he has to send it in by drone." The Specter said.

"Will I have contact with him?" Craig asked.

"No one will. His asset status is unknown to even him. He thinks he is freelancing. I will return him to you in due time." A gravelly sound that may have been a chuckle emitted from behind the mask. "He is a fool, but his video will provide the necessary intelligence. His falling in with the Mountain Warriors is a fortuitous mistake, but do not feel like I forgive you. I never forget incompetence."

"Why are you so interested in the destruction of the Mountain Posers?" Craig asked.

"Their destruction is up to you. We are only interested in them leading us to what is ours."

"And what is your specific interest? I know you are not altruistic," Craig asked.

"Don't sweat it," The Specter said as he handed Craig a backpack.

Craig hefted it and seemed satisfied with the weight. He held it like a treasure.

"What are you getting out of our meetings?" Craig asked again.

"I will see you, same time, same day, next week unless something happens. I may stop by your town tomorrow." With that said, The Specter turned and walked back into the dark forest.

Craig glared at The Specter's broad back as he disappeared into the gloom. Craig wondered about the point of these meetings. His wonder disappeared when he unzipped the bag and looked inside. A smile slashed his face. It was protein powder and steroids. Most important were the fourteen packets of what he called, "The magic powder." It kept Craig alive.

| 13 |

Despite the wonder of what was in store for me in the morning, I slept like a boulder at the base of a cliff. My mind eased with the revelation that the tribe didn't hold me in suspicion. I felt that if Bryan held me in a higher regard, the others would easily follow.

The morning greeted me with the chirping of birds and weak light seeping in through the spaces between the tarps. I snuggled in my bedding. The sleeping bag seemed to entice me to stay inside like a warm motherly embrace. My face was the only part of me exposed to the cold air and feeling the contrast between my cold face versus the cocoon warmth of the bag, it was an easy decision to remain as I was.

Next, I heard at least two babies or toddlers crying with some mothers quietly cooing them.

Shortly afterwards, I heard men discussing the plans of the day in a quiet manner to avoid waking the kids or maybe to avoid attracting enemies. Despite straining, I couldn't hear everything they said, but the voices of the men told me these were tough guys. It wasn't in the volume or what they said, but rather in the sober determined cadence. Every word said was necessary and meant.

Next, I could hear some pots and pans clanging, and I soon smelled the smoky campfires getting stoked. Shortly after, I could smell meat cooking with the aroma of heavy garlic. I assumed it was deer meat. Despite being a vegetarian, my mouth watered. I was about to crawl out of the sleeping bag when I heard the sharp report of someone striking the tarp wall in the rhythm someone would use to knock on the door to the tune of "Shave and a haircut."

"Eric." I heard Bryan call.

For some reason I didn't immediately answer, maybe a fear of facing the uncertainties in my new life.

"Listen, I know you're in there. I see no fresh footprints leaving your hovel. You awake, man? It's late in the morning."

I suddenly felt self-conscious for sleeping in. "Yeah, I am awake," Guiltily, I tried to brighten my voice to attempt to sound as wide awake as possible. "Come in if you want."

The sun caused me to squint as Bryan flung the tarp aside and poked his head in. "Greet the sun and break the fast. We have a busy day today."

Before I finished nodding, Bryan had slammed the tarp back in place and went on about his business.

I had slept in my clothes. So, I sat up and slapped on my boots and immediately made my way to the communal fire. It was kept small to avoid burning the tarp that stretched between four trees by parachute cord to protect it from rainstorms.

Anna smiled and greeted me saying, "We have venison for breakfast."

Her two young children ran and played near the fire with the parents giving them very little attention. The one-year old baby hung from her mother's trunk by some kind of a wrap. The kids looked very lean with slightly hollowed eyes and cheeks, but had a vitality that I had rarely seen in kids outside of the Forbidden Zone.

My stomach growled like a hungry lion would roar. The garlic and the meat were getting to me. I almost desired to give up vegetarianism.

I jumped as a heavy hand slapped my back. "Dig in," said Bryan.

I looked at the venison that he offered me on a metal plate and asked, "Got anything that's vegetarian?"

"There are people nearby who would kill for what you are turning your nose up at," Bryan said as if insulted by the rejection.

Scott piped in from behind me, "Vegetarian? Gee, Eric, I didn't know you were..." He let the sentence trail off as he held his hand up in a prone position and rocked it back and forth as if attempting to maintain a level but failing. His implication was obvious. He was questioning my manhood or sexuality over my dietary choices. Probably both, because I guessed that he was trying to press any button he could. I also noted that his English grammar was near perfect as he knew that would not offend me like it would Bryan. His taunt didn't bother me in itself, but the schoolyard nature struck me as so purposefully petty, that I found myself infuriated, Anna as well.

"Scott!" Anna scolded sharply.

"I love it when you say my name like that, sweetie." Scott said with his stupid laugh.

"Scott, be polite to our guest," Anna said.

"I was, darling," Scott said with a smarmy smile. "I was celebrating his coming out."

"I am not..." I started and stopped. Again, this felt too much like sixth grade.

"It's OK Eric," she said.

"Yeah, it's OK, Eric," Scott said laughing. "See even Anna agrees that you should be who you are."

"Forget it," I said.

Bryan rubbed the bridge of his nose. I couldn't tell if he was laughing at Scott or was angry at him for talking to his wife and me like that. I guessed that it may have been a combination. As I said, a person could laugh out loud just looking at the goofy fat guy and his way of saying everything like a joke, even if he simultaneously grated on your nerves.

"You can eat the wild onions that we used for flavoring." Bryan suggested deadpan. I wasn't sure if he was being serious or sarcastic because sometimes people are mystified by what a vegetarian consumes to survive.

I watched as Bryan picked up a pot of water that he was heating for tea. I had quickly learned that any kind of tea was vital in the winter. Not only did it warm the hands and body, but a lot of warmth was lost with each exhale. Inhaling the warm steam from a cup held directly under the mouth and nose was about as good as drinking the hot liquid.

"Seriously?" I asked not reading him as usual.

"Seriously. In case you didn't notice, we're a bit limited up here. Unless you plan on converting to breathatarian--" Bryan said and he added some brownish powder to the hot water. He stirred it up as it thickened.

"Breath-a-who?" asked Scott.

"Lives on breathing alone," Bryan answered and then spoke to me, raising his voice to speak over Scott who continued to mumble his usual nonsense, "I hate to tell you this, but you're going to have to drastically change your diet, my friend."

Scott whistled and said, "Dagum. I heard of not living on bread alone, but you gotta go full ridiculousness if you think you can live on breath alone."

Bryan shrugged in reply and said to Scott, "There are all kinds out there, man."

"I can eat eggs," I said as I eyed a few of the chickens that ran free range in the camp.

"Sorry, Eric," Anna said with true compassion. "They quit laying in the winter, especially with that lack of regular food."

"On rare occasions I can eat fish," I offered with what I thought was a reasonable concession.

I glared at Scott as he burst out laughing with his head in his hands like he just heard the stupidest thing ever. He stopped laughing and looked at me and then laughed harder.

"What?" I demanded.

Scott kept on laughing and said in a horrible mock British accent, "I say govenah, just let me get my yacht and we'll go out on the ocean a few hundred miles away and catch you some swordfish and maybe some caviar and then—and then we'll stop by some café or some such thing and order some champagne and then--." He was laughing so hard that he couldn't finish.

"Do you have to be such an ass?" I demanded.

I was worried that he would dish out some reprisal. I steeled my body in anticipation for a punch, but instead he did something worse. He patted me on the head and ruffled my hair as he would have patronized a child.

"Relax," Scott said with a lighter laugh. "Your Uncle Scott is just messing with you."

I punched his arm away from me and stood up. I now seriously wanted a fight. My already injured knuckle struck his elbow when I swung at him, and despite thinking that I broke my hand, I held my fists up ready to fight. I knew how to fight. I was ready to show them.

"Don't touch me," I raged.

"Damn, my funny bone." He said rubbing his elbow. I could see the anger rising in him like a liquid. He looked at me as if the anger in his body reached eyeball level as his face reddened. "Listen, son— "he said sternly.

"I am not your son." I felt fear creeping back into me. I still stood my ground, but I was afraid that if he struck me, my bravado would melt.

He stepped towards me raising his fist in anger.

"Scott!" Anna yelled

"What?" he asked her, keeping his increasingly belligerent gaze on me.

"Get out of here and leave him alone," she demanded as she pointed in a general direction away from the communal campfire.

"I am just funnin' with the kid," he said.

"He's not having fun, you idiot," she said firmly without raising her voice, but with gritted teeth.

He started to open his mouth, but she interrupted him and shook her head. "Uh uh. Leave," she ordered as she continued pointing in a general direction away from me.

I looked over at Bryan. He was absently stirring his pot as his eyes were focused widely on the situation rather than any individual. It seemed he was just studying, determining who passed a test. I didn't know if I did pass the test or if the test was even over.

"Yes ma'am," Scott said amicably and left. He cut across the camp and started joking with another member of the group. I tried to note who, but everyone looked alike: scruffy to the Nth degree.

Anna took me by the elbow and said calmly as if the drama between Scott and I never happened, "Deer meat and wild onions are all we have cooked, and I am sorry, but it's probably the only food within five miles of the camp as well."

"What about nuts, berries, roots, or leaves?" I asked.

Bryan smirked as if he already won a debate. He reminded me of Han Solo talking to Princess Leia as he confidently pointed to the wilderness around the camp and confidently said, "Look around us."

I looked into the forest and raised my hands in questioning shrug. "What?"

"What do you see?" he prompted as he stirred his pot.

I looked. This time I saw the landscape through a survivor's eyes. The world before me was the typical winter landscape and I now understood my dilemma. There was not a single, green leaf, berry or nut upon tree, shrub, or herb. All I could see were cold naked trees and a carpet of dead leaves on the forest floor.

"Most greens and berries are out of season," Bryan said as I looked around. "What is still green is mostly poisonous. There are some nuts and roots buried in the leaves under the nut trees, but the trees in this grove are all poplars and maples," Bryan said with a hint of compassion, but he mainly delivered it as if he were simply giving a lecture. I found out later that before it all went down that he would occasionally lead people on foraging expeditions for wild edible plants.

"Where are the nut trees?" I asked as I continued to look around at the stark landscape. All the barren trees looked the same to me with their grey bark and withered branches vainly reaching above for the cold heavens.

He waved his hands toward the distance. "About a mile away is a big grove of hickory. However, it may defeat your purpose as a vegetarian."

"Why is that?" I asked.

"At this point in the season they're infested with weevil larva. So, anything of nutritional value in the nut shell is technically an animal. However, in their defense, the worms do make a delicious meal in themselves."

I responded by making a face and then asked, "What about wild roots?"

"There are a bunch," said Anna, "but a lot of them are rare and we only dig them for very dire emergencies. A lot of them have medicinal qualities and should be eaten in minimal amounts. Shelley can fill you in on them better than anyone."

"All that environmentalism aside," Bryan said, ever the pragmatist, "The herbaceous tops have died back due to the winter. You need to have a sharp eye for the ecological environment, companion plants, and to be able to recognize the brown remains of those certain plants. And that's if the dead remains haven't been trampled and blown away."

"How were vegetarians able to eat in the old days?" I asked.

Bryan laughed, not mockingly but with sympathy, "Outside of the tropics, veganism is a modern fad. There were no vegan cultures in northern climes until back before the zombie outbreak when they could ship stuff in from southern shores during the winter."

"You looked starved," Anna said in a motherly tone. "Get something to eat before these cheeks of yours get any hollower. When we get a cold spell, you'll be wishing for any layer of fat to keep you warm."

I reached tentatively to grab a bit of deer meat, when Bryan said, "Hold up, brother."

He handed me the pot that he had stirred. I received it by the handle and saw a brown gruel.

"What is this?" I asked.

"White oak acorns cooked as porridge," he proclaimed.

"I thought they were poisonous."

"Mmmm, not quite poisonous," he said. "They have high amounts of tannic acid in them. It's a decent antiseptic. We leach that out by boiling them in a few changes of water. That water, we reduce down and add it to our homemade hand sanitizer."

"Thanks," I said.

"Don't thank me," he chuckled, "until you try it. We reserve it to feed the chickens through the winter, or eat it ourselves during times of extreme famine."

I tried a hesitant bite. It wasn't bad, but it wasn't great either. It tasted simply nourishing, with salt and garlic. Like a savory grits without butter or cheese.

"Not bad for chicken food. It's very garlicky," I said.

"Shelley is an herbalist. We're not sure how the zombie virus, bacteria, whatever is spread," Bryan admitted, "but she says that garlic is good for the immune system. So, we go crazy over it."

I ate a few more bites. I was quickly acquiring a taste for garlic acorn grits. "Thanks," I said again now that I had fully tasted them.

"Don't sweat it. I occasionally experiment with vegetarianism, mostly to cleanse the system, and of course to get the attention of vegetarian chicks," he said as he winked at his wife.

I nodded as I had my mouth too full to speak, but I smiled at his joke. Jennifer was a vegetarian. I had been loyal to this diet for the last year because of our relationship. Giving up on the vegetarian lifestyle felt like I was letting go of not just her but my whole civilized life.

Bryan grew serious and asked, "By the way, what do they think is the cause of this zombie outbreak? You know, outside of here, where you are from?"

Everybody at one time or another would ask me pointedly about what was being done on the outside or hoped I would divulge some inside scoop on what caused the infection. Even if they had heard me answer already, they seemed to think that I was holding back information and that if they buddied up, I could reveal more, but even being on friendly terms with Tommy and my uncle, I felt as in the dark as these guys in the Forbidden Zone.

I shrugged and said through a mouthful of gritty acorns. "I don't know if they studied it. They are scared to death. I mean, they were about to literally shoot and incinerate me at the fence. They don't know anything."

"I doubt that. Someone knows something and they aren't saying a damn thing. Probably for fear of incriminating themselves." Bryan said with a heart burning bitterness that he had kept hidden until this moment. Bryan turned to leave and said without looking at me, "I'm going to get you a present. Follow me when you finish eating."

"I'll tell you what the cause of the zombie disease is," Scott yelled.

I looked at him annoyed for coming back into the conversation, but he did look like he had something of value to add.

"What is it?" I asked.

Scott seriously opined, "It was caused by mass consumption of CBD oil, but there is a potential cure..."

"Really? What's that?" I asked.

"Eating lots of gluten, of course," he answered. He held my serious gaze until I started laughing and he joined in as well.

"Get out of here Scott," Anna instructed with a roll of her eyes.

Anna looked at me when Bryan and Scott were out of earshot and said, "Bryan thinks the government designed it."

"Do you agree," I asked.

"What do you think?" the bitterness that suddenly welled up in her voice told me her thoughts. As she said that, her hand shot out and adroitly caught her son a split second before he ran into the campfire. "Watch yourself!" she scolded as she swatted him on the butt.

"Ow!" he screamed back.

"The fire will hurt a lot worse. Now watch yourself," she scolded.

The boy gave her a dirty look and then went back to playing as if nothing happened.

"I don't mean to critique your parenting, but they get awfully close to the fire. Isn't there a fence or something that you can put around it?"

She shook her head, "there are no protective fences or warning labels. That's a fantasy of the past. Bryan and I live by the code of 'No rules, just consequences.' Granted we protect them from serious injury, death, and zombies, but sometimes mistakes are the best way to learn. It teaches responsibility." She paused and looked directly at me. "That applies equally to you. Be careful today. A mistake doesn't just endanger you, but this whole tribe."

I kept eating and nodded with confidence. Inside, I shrugged her warning off. The worst I figured that would happen was that I would learn how to throw a knife at a stump. I was safely ensconced in a mountain tribe of warriors. There was no way I would be wielding a blade like Conan the Barbarian slaying the hordes of the undead, I naively assumed.

"Be careful," she said again.

I didn't let my irritation for being treated like a child register on my face. I quickly finished the last mouthfuls and followed in the direction that Bryan had taken. I came to a small clearing on the other side of camp. I entered and attempted to put on an air of confidence for whatever awaited.

| 14 |

There were three men training in the clearing. None of them stopped to acknowledge me. One was a thin young man, maybe 19 years old with something like a beard that resembled the rags for clothes that hung from his boney frame. I learned his name was Robert. Underneath the beard was an intense and serious face. He seemed to favor a slightly injured leg as he wrestled with that knife throwing trapper, Critter. It appeared less of a competition, but rather like Critter was giving the kid a lesson.

I watched for a moment. The two grapplers stopped to stare at the third man who was training. I instantly recognized him by his screams.

That third man was Scott. With his Louisville Slugger, he beat the crap out of a few posts. He cursed it with silly expletives about various relations of the posts and their exotic and impossible fetishes. He would scream, loud outrageous 'Wahs!' like a Bruce Lee movie. He would do clumsy, over-dramatic rolls and attacks, but beneath the goofiness, I could tell the man was purposely hiding some danger.

"Keep quiet, Scott, you'll draw the horde," Adam yelled in his commanding old man's voice from across camp.

Scott quieted down, a little, but kept up the antics.

The other men were laughing, and soon I was too. Despite the way he dished out teasing and insults to others, Scott was even more ruthless when he made fun of himself. He made points about his own weight, age, and rough exterior.

When Scott saw me, he brushed himself off with a comical air of dignity.

"You taught that post a lesson," I said.

He extended his hand, and I shook it with a mischievous smile as if I was about to deliver a punchline.

"I done saw that post checking out my girlfriend. It was immediately after I made passionate love to her," he said. With the needless addition of the word "done," I definitely felt that he was setting up for a joke.

I tried to disengage from shaking his hand; it was almost at that awkward stage, so I asked the obvious question, "You have a girlfriend?"

"Yer shaking her," he said smiling in my face and gripping my hand tighter.

I yanked my hand out of his grasp and wiped it on my pants. The men around me laughed and I joined as well.

"This is Critter," Scott introduced the other man.

"I know him," I said.

"You obviously don't," Scott contradicted. Before I could argue, Scott laughed, "If you really knew him, you would have walked the other way when you first spotted him."

The laughter was more polite and less from the belly, this time.

Scott then pointed to the younger man, "This here is Robert, but don't call ole Bobby here Bob, Robby or any variation because Jim Bob doesn't like it. Ain't that right Bobby?"

I shook Robert's hand. He laughed, but I could see his eyes were as intense as when he wrestled with Critter.

We exchanged greetings and then I lifted up my camera and asked if I could interview them. They agreed.

"So," I started, "this was called the Mountain Warriors seminar before it all went down. What type of martial arts do you specialize in, Critter?

He shrugged, "A variety. When I found a hole in one art that I couldn't ignore, I'd try another one until I found a hole, and so on, never excessively loyal to anything. I was a bit of a dojo slut."

"What about you Scott?"

"I'm the GrandMaster of Hung Kung Fuey! Wah!" Scott screamed like Bruce Lee and performed a goofy jumping kick. "Joking aside, I was just a student. Mostly I just whack the bastards with this baseball bat."

"He whacks, pretty good," said Critter with a deadpan expression.

"Thanks," said Scott. "I whack the bastards good," he said again with a Babe Ruth swing of the bat.

"Why not a sword?" I asked.

"Less bloody. I don't want their ocher on my fine clothes," he said as he ran his hands down his rags.

"What do you do?" I asked Robert.

"As little as possible," Scott answered for him.

"Scott, let Robert speak," Critter lightly scolded.

Robert spoke up, "Grand Master Adam taught me a variety of stuff that he had learned over the years. You really should interview him. He's a walking encyclopedia on martial arts and life in general."

"I will," I assured him, "but he keeps escaping me. How long have you studied with him?"

"Not long. Bobby's still wet behind the ears as a—"

"That's enough foolishness, Scott!" I snapped. My desire for a professional quality documentary overrode any fear of causing bad feelings among the group, especially with Scott.

Scott was about to protest, but as he looked at the face of Critter and Robert he could see that they agreed with me.

I looked at Robert and asked again, "How long?"

"Not long. Maybe a year before the quarantine. I've been training here ever since." He looked down and said, "I am not very good."

"He was going to join the Marines." Scott said. When I gave Scott a dirty look, he replied, "I'm being serious. I served in the Marines and Robert was serious about going in too, had it not all gone down. I respect that in him."

Critter spoke up, "How does wanting to go in mean you're something. I wanted to join and didn't."

"Yeah," agreed Scott, "you weren't serious. This kid was and would have. Everyone was telling him he was dumb or crazy, including me, but he persisted. That kid has heart."

"Why would you persist when people call you names for wanting to join?" I asked.

"To defend my country's freedom," said Robert.

"A lot of freedom our country gives us now," Critter said bitterly.

"I said I wanted to join to defend my freedom, too," Scott said, "but in retrospect, I was twenty-two. They said I was a man, but everyone still treated me like a goofy kid. My goal was to prove otherwise."

"No," said Robert. "I really wanted to defend—"

"Yeah right, kid," said Scott with a laugh.

Robert opened his mouth to protest, his chest puffed out slightly, and anger lit his eyes.

Scott laughed, "See, you want to be taken seriously, right"

Robert's offensive stance seemed to melt. Scott had pegged him and he knew it.

Scott continued, "I learned early that no one was gonna take me seriously. No one does now, so screw 'em. Have fun in life."

Everyone chuckled.

At that moment Bryan seemed to appear before me. I looked him in the eyes. He had a seriousness to him that I hadn't quite seen before. The best word I could use to describe his seriousness would be the word: Ceremonial.

He said, "Here is my gift. It is yours."

I looked at what was in his hands with a bit of awe. I could feel my own hands tremble.

"It's a little bigger than your multi-tool blade," Bryan said with a hint of sarcasm.

He reverentially offered me a katana in its shiny black lacquered scabbard. The sword lay across his two extended hands, his head was bowed slightly, the curve of the blade pointed at him.

"Thanks," I said. I tried picking up the sword with the same reverence that he displayed toward me, but I was in awe and felt clumsy.

"You've never held a sword, have you?" Bryan asked.

"Aside from a toy one, no," I joked. I didn't tell them that I spent many weekends fighting with padded swords. I knew that I couldn't swing this one the same way because I knew this one would cause damage. It was like how the vampire girl affected me in my dreams; I was both excited and fearful.

"I can tell. Your hands are trembling," he said.

"I guess I respect the blade," I said.

"No. That's fear that causes the tremor, but we'll turn it into respect."

"What's the difference," I asked.

Bryan explained, "You should fear nothing. Not even your own death. However, you should have respect for everyone and everything. For instance, I don't fear Critter. However, I respect him deeply. If I lose my respect for him and abuse him or underestimate him, he'll quickly introduce me to pain and that will reintroduce me to my fear."

"I see. That's deep," I said.

"That ain't him saying that," said Scott. "That's Grand Masta Adam."

Bryan continued, "Someone who fears a blade can learn to respect it and become a great swordsman. Someone with no fear, who sees it as a toy, may never have the proper respect and is in danger of hurting himself with it. Then the fear will come if he's lucky to survive his self inflicted stupidity. Then maybe he can gain the respect. So relax your shoulders. That's where you're carrying your fear."

I realized that my shoulders were indeed tight and high up my neck as if protecting my head. I loosened them.

After a pause, as I digested his words, Bryan said. "Pull the sword out of the scabbard respectfully. Keep your muscles relaxed."

I did as respectfully as I could. It was beautiful. The handle was wrapped in a black ribbon. The blade gleamed like the sun, but it was short. Most of the swords that I saw were about three feet long. This was only two feet long.

I gently touched the blade a few times and said, "It's not that sharp. I then ran my finger over a few inches of the length and it easily drew blood. "Whoa," I exclaimed, jerking it away and sucking on the wound.

"A sword is meant to slice, not hack." Bryan instructed.

When he saw me looking at my scratch he said, "Never mind the blood. That's not the first your blade has tasted."

I let that sink in and said, "Thanks, and this isn't a complaint, just an observation—"

"The sword is short?" Bryan finished for me.

"It's always about the size, length and width, ain't it," Scott commented with his hinting smile.

I nodded to Bryan without a smile, not giving Scott the pleasure. I simply ignored his crude attempt at a joke.

"It's called a wakizashi, the little brother of a katana." Bryan then assured me, "You'll find you have more control in tight quarters."

"Like a small room?" I asked.

"That and if we're standing on a line defending ourselves from a horde, you won't accidentally slice your brother or sister beside you."

I protested, "As a journalist, I'm an impartial observer. I would rather not wield a blade against anyone human or undead."

"Then you'll be an impartial brain on a zombie's dinner plate." Scott said. Judging by how heartily the others laughed, I guessed that Scott had spoken an ultimate truth. I noticed with Scott, if he joked about the truth, it was followed by a belly laugh or the evil eye. There were no in between reactions.

"Scott's right," Bryan said. "Everyone has to pull his weight."

As they spoke, it was almost like the blade came alive in my hands and stood upright, blade pointing to the heavens. It was my muscles that moved it of course, but at that moment it was like my instincts decided to learn the way of the blade. I nodded my understanding to them and said, "I will learn and stand with you, then. I give you my solemn word."

I meant it. My statement may look cheesy on paper, but the men could see the determination in my eyes. They nodded seriously.

Bryan took the scabbard and let me keep the blade. He led me to the post that Scott had attacked earlier. The post was more of a dead sapling with some give to it when struck.

"Slice it," he said.

I took a few tentative hacks like swinging an axe or a baseball bat like Scott, but Bryan startled me by placing his hand gently on my arm. I stopped swinging and looked at him as he explained a scenario.

"Swing at it like you are in battle. That post represents five brain eaters and you have to strike them down before they kill you. Right now, you look like a wuss. You wouldn't last five seconds. Literally."

I looked at the post and felt the fear as if I was literally fighting for my life. I was already trying to swing hard but when Bryan insulted me, I felt a rage rise above my fear. I swung for the fences. I hit it hard, but the blade bounced off because of my grip. I didn't have the blade at a flush angle. I corrected it and my blade sank deep into the wood so that it stuck.

"The blade is stuck in one brain eater's skulls," Bryan yelled in a deep, loud commanding voice that I didn't think he was capable of doing. "Pull it out quick before another one gets you. Or you will join them."

I yanked hard a few times in a panic. On the third try the blade sprang free and almost hit me. I fell. Before I could stand back up, Bryan screamed.

"They're still attacking. Cut their legs out from under them. Keep swinging from the ground or you're dead!"

I swung weakly from the ground. I could not find a solid position to launch an attack.

"Keep swinging, but stand up as you do," he commanded, "or they'll pile on top of you!

I did, but it was awkward as hell as I moved quickly in a spasmodic panic. I could either get up or I could swing. It was impossible to do both, but I tried, getting to a sitting, kneeling and finally to a standing position. Once on my feet, I swung a few more times before Bryan said in a quieter and calmer voice, "Stop, stop, stop, stop."

It wasn't until the fourth 'stop' that my brain registered the command. I stopped and bent over with my hands on my knees. I was glad that I didn't brag about my sword fighting in the park with the padded swords. I was well aware that I looked like a klutz.

"Not bad as far as heart goes. You got a lot of heart, Eric," said Critter.

"But," I prompted.

"But you ain't got no talent," said Scott. "Hell, you looked like me playing with my pecker." Scott laughed and raised his arms up and down like he was rubbing his hands up and down a ten foot flag pole.

Bryan chuckled, "Crude but accurate. A few quick things: You only swung the blade thirty times. You're out of breath because you held it for the first fifteen swings. In combat, take a breath before your first swing and let it go immediately and keep breathing."

"I know about breathing," I confidently said, "I took yoga for a while."

He pursed his lips as if to say, no comment and then continued his critique. "Holding your breath is a sign that every muscle is tense including the diaphragm. This plants your feet, you lose your mobility and that's why you fell. Your stiffness is why you couldn't find a foundation on the ground to attack."

The other men were quiet, and I could see by subtle nods that they were in agreement.

"Finally, the rule in swordplay is that the pointy end always, always points at the bad guy."

"Well duh," I joked.

"Then why didn't you do it?" Scott asked.

I cast him an irritated look, but everyone else was in agreement with him. I opened my mouth to respond, but Bryan took away my sword and gave me a practice wooden sword. Without being told, Critter picked up another wooden sword. A smile cut his otherwise morose features. I could tell that I was going to have to fight or at least spar with him.

"Breathe out, now," Bryan said. "That gasp is fear and that will cause you to freeze when you need to fight."

I blew the air out of my lungs with disgust. I realized I tensed at the idea of doing a drill with the tracker. I hated how Bryan always seemed more aware of the state of my body than I was.

"Now," Bryan instructed, "attack Critter like you attacked the post."

I looked at both men incredulously.

"Come on," said Critter. "I love this stuff." He smiled even bigger.

I was about to gently swing at him, when Bryan said with a mocking laugh "Swing at him. You couldn't hurt him even if you wanted. Breathe out with a war cry."

Again the insult to my manhood.

I felt a rage as if I was savagely smacked across the face. With a scream, I launched myself at Critter, who nimbly dodged and blocked. He easily could have struck me back with his wooden sword, but instead he gave me a polite tap with it.

"He won't hit you back. Now attack like you have a pair," Bryan instructed.

I launched a barrage with everything I had. Critter kept smiling bigger and bigger. His eyes were bright and full of life as he evaded and blocked. Each time he could have done either one, but he did both combined. Each of his evasions placed him in a better position where he could have easily killed me if he wanted.

"Breathe out! War cry!" said Bryan.

I roared.

Critter smiled and lowered his sword, giving me an easy target at the top of his head. I was so enraged at his skill and mocking smile. I brought the sword up and far back to give a death blow, but before I could bring it down on him, he dropped his sword, seemed to appear inches from my face with his smile, a small knife to my throat, his other hand stopped the butt of my sword from arching over to slice him. He held my sword in place and he asked me, "Who is the pointy end pointing at?"

The blade was over my head pointing at the ground behind me, in Bryan's general direction, not Critter's.

"I see," I said with defeat. "Pointy end at the bad guy, not pointy end at the ground behind me. I wasted it on an exaggerated wind up."

"Hold yer head up, kid," Scott said. "You may miss in skill, but you got some heart. You can always learn skill, but you can't learn heart."

"Scott's right. I can see it in your eyes," said Bryan.

"Sorry, for attacking you Critter." I said, suddenly conscious of my fury even as harmless as I was against a superior warrior.

"Never apologize for not hurting me. We should thank each other for making us stronger. In the future, as you become more deadly, please use a little more control. I'd rather not get my wig split."

I smiled back at him, "You got it, brothers." It was weird. I was still an outcast to my world and an outsider to this tribe, yet somehow I felt a closeness, a bond with Critter, Bryan, Robert, and even Scott just from the short swordplay.

They smiled and nodded back.

"Now watch Critter." Bryan said as he pointed to my wakizashi.

Critter picked up my sword and I was startled as Bryan attacked him swiftly with a wooden sword, but yet Bryan was calm enough to explain. "Watch how Critter blocks and twists the handle so I don't hit the sharp blade and damage it. He makes sure his block is with the flat side of the sword." Bryan's wooden sword struck like lightning from the sky. Each time, Critter brought my sword up slanted down like a roof so that Bryan's sword slid down like rain water. Bryan continued his instruction when he was sure I had understood what I had seen. "Watch how I can't hit his body because whether he is slashing or blocking, the blade stays in front and is always pointed in my direction. I can't get through his defense because he always keeps the blade between us. He never takes it out of the game to wind up for a swing. His wind up is short and almost unnoticed."

Bryan withheld anymore blows and told Critter, "Slash the pole."

Critter attacked the pole with a savagery that I hoped I would never face. Chips of wood from his slices floated to the ground like snowflakes.

Bryan continued, "See how his blows have no wind up. He strikes from where the blade is. His parries and blocks serve as his wind up. Also notice that his strikes are harder than yours despite the lack of wind up. Also, he's not getting his blade stuck, do you see why?"

"Yes," I answered. It was like I could see every mistake that I made, but it didn't discourage me. Instead I couldn't wait for my chance to train and correct my mistakes. I answered Bryan, "I see that he doesn't hit with the sword, but rather it slides, or slices. It's like how I cut my finger."

Indeed Critter's cuts were deeper, but the blade slid out as easily as a serpent glides through the grass.

"Good," then Bryan instructed Critter, "Keep attacking but go to the ground and get back up to your feet a few times."

Bryan looked at me and said, "This is important, to learn to move while attacking or defending. You'll trip over bodies or slip on blood when on a battlefield. You may also have to drop to the ground immediately to dodge a blow."

I watched in awe as Critter continued his attack from any position, sitting, kneeling, standing, crouching, even lying, he could launch a deadly strike with the sword. No matter his posture, even moving from one position to another, the blade bit deep into the wooden pole with his slashes. Indeed every subtle movement acted like a wind up. Because it was natural movement, it didn't look like a wind up and his deadliness was always hidden.

Bryan pointed out a few keys that I was noticing, "Watch how he finds the structure in his body to deliver a powerful slash no matter what position he's in, or even in between any of those positions."

I noticed that not only was Critter good, but he was thoroughly enjoying the movement. His focus was so sharp on the attacks that he became locked in his world. He was good and he knew it.

"Damn," I swore with reverence at what I saw.

However, Critter's pride came crashing down as Bryan struck him with the wooden sword as Critter rolled to a squatting position. Bryan swung at full speed and pulled back at the last moment. Critter brought my wakizashi sword up to block, but it was too late. The wooden sword made contact with Critter's head with a solid thunk. I could tell that it hurt, but he resisted rubbing his head. Was it out of stoicism or pride? I didn't know.

Bryan said in a mildly condescending voice, "All that good skill is worthless if you get tunnel vision. There will usually be more than one attacker. Always keep your peripheral vision open."

Critter stood up and faced Bryan. He didn't seem hurt, but I could see something didn't sit right with him. He said, "Thanks for the reminder," but his eyes blazed.

"That's a lot to keep in mind. How will I remember all that in combat?" I asked.

"You won't," said Critter. "It must be ingrained."

I looked at him curiously.

Bryan answered, "That's why you're going to practice all hours, every day until we're satisfied that you will be an asset and not a liability."

"How about just giving me a gun so I can defeat a swordsman..." I tried to imitate Indiana Jones calmly pulling a gun on a swordsman and shooting.

Scott joked, "Untrained with a sword, you are only dangerous to a friend at four feet away. I wouldn't feel safe within a few miles of you if you held a firearm."

No one laughed, but the men nodded in agreement. Robert, who was usually silent, was the only one who said anything with a drawled out, "yep."

I did not like being looked at like an imbecile. Even the nineteen year old kid, Robert, didn't think much about me.

Bryan added, "Besides, if you weren't smart enough to enter this quarantined area armed with a firearm, you'll have to wait to find someone who trusts you enough to sell you one."

"How much would one cost?"

Bryan replied, "Here you need skills or hard assets. You have neither. So I suggest you start training."

"If you don't like training, you can always sell that ass of yours to the Low Boys," Scott laughed.

"I think I'd rather be a swordsman," I said.

"Good choice," Scott replied.

"Critter will help you. I have to go speak to Adam," Bryan said. "The Specter is scoping us out from the hills above. He has seemed very interested in us since you arrived."

I looked around for The Specter, but Critter scolded.

"Don't act suspicious."

As we watched Bryan walk away, I caught Critter in the corner of my eye rubbing the spot where Bryan hit him in the head. It amazed me how he resisted rubbing it for so long. It seemed people would rather show stoicism than their pain. I couldn't help but wonder if it was a bunch of macho baloney or if it was essential to survival. Maybe in this broken age of constant pain and sorrow, there wasn't any point in showing what was always present. It would be tiring to hear people complain about the obvious constantly, however, there would have been no stopping me from complaining if someone whacked me over the head with a wooden sword.

I then practiced for a few hours with Critter, Scott, and Robert. Eventually I could see the tracker was getting bored.

He looked to make sure anyone who would object was out of earshot. Then Critter turned to me, "Screw that. You wanna learn about firearms?"

"Uh, yeah," I said.

I watched him pull his handgun from his waist. He did it in a smooth way as he brought his hips smoothly to meet his reaching hand at the halfway point. I tried to calm the tension in my body as Bryan instructed when I was introduced to my sword, but I could feel my hands start to shake in anticipation.

Critter explained the working parts as he pressed a button, released a magazine and pulled it out of the handgun. He slid the top part of the handgun back, emptied a bullet out of the chamber. He stated that it was unloaded and looked into the chamber. He pointed out that you knew it was unloaded because you could see daylight streaming through the barrel in the chamber of the gun, meaning there was no bullet. He then placed the magazine back into the gun and explained how he chambered a round as he slid the top back and let it slide back with a crack that sounded to me almost as loud as a gunshot. I learned that it was a very strong spring that slammed the slide back into place.

He then looked me square in the eyes for emphasis and asked, "Do you know the first and most important rule of firearms?"

I was about to say, you don't talk about fight club, but I could tell humor wouldn't be accepted. Even Scott looked serious.

I finally said, "I don't know."

"Never point a gun at anyone, even if you think it's unloaded unless you mean to destroy the thing that you point at. Never use a gun's barrel to point or direct. Too many people have been shot by an 'unloaded' gun." He did finger quotes for "unloaded." "And keep your booger picker off the trigger unless you want this to go boom. Got it?"

I nodded and then I said a very affirmative, "Yes."

He handed the handgun to me and I received it. If the sword caused me to tremble, this was like the San Andreas Fault dropped California in the Pacific Ocean. I had never really seen a gun other than seeing one holstered on a cop. That may have been one of the reasons why Don and the border guards scared the crap out of me.

"Relax. Breathe," Critter instructed.

"Yeah, man," Scott said. "Get a hold of yourself."

I looked at the joker and he wasn't joking around.

Scott cracked a grin after a moment, "You're a North East Coast liberal, ain't you."

I smiled back trying to look brave, but it was probably a grimace. "I admit that I was always for gun control in the past."

"Now?" asked Scott.

"I think I was correct in that situation back then, but now, I guess I am an NRA member," I joked.

Scott shook his head and said, "Naw. They're too liberal. We're all GOA."

I didn't know what he was talking about, but I felt in no position to say anything, so I just nodded.

"Damn, right," said Scott.

For some reason it struck me as funny and I laughed. We all did for a moment.

We sobered and I looked at the three of them and said, "It's weird. I started the day scared, an outcast. I know you guys don't fully trust me, but just after the bit of sword and gun stuff, I feel like you are all my brothers. I've never truly understood the camaraderie of soldiers and stuff until now.

"Brothers of the swords and guns. Mountain Warriors," Scott shouted the phrase Mountain Warriors in a slightly goofy manner. I guessed it was getting too sappy for him, but it didn't matter. This felt like my tribe.

"By default," Critter explained, "every martial artist is my friend."

I curiously cocked my head.

He continued, "No one just comes up and hits me unless they want their ass kicked. You have to be a very good friend of mine for me to let you hit me, like Bryan when he hit me with the wooden sword. I was angry for a second. Had it been someone else, they would have been sprawled on the floor. However, Bryan is a brother and taught me something. There is no room for grudges between us. So anyone I train with or will train with is my friend." He paused and looked at me and said, "That includes you."

He then directed me to unload the gun and talked me through reloading it. I slid the top back and let it slide home chambering a round. It was ready to fire. The shakes were gone. I felt confident. Alive. I held the power of life and death in my hand.

Scott yelled, "Stop!"

The gun seemed to explode in my hand and all hell let loose.

| 15 |

It seemed the gunshot echoed twice as long as those reverbed gunshots on the Spaghetti Westerns. When the gun fell out of my hand, I realized I had accidently pulled the trigger.

"You idiot!" said Scott, shaking his head. I didn't think that clown could show such anger. His face had reddened and his jaw clenched so that I could see the masseter muscles.

Every eye in the little village was on me. People came from every corner to stare at us.

The kid, Robert, was the first to scold, "And that's why you never point the gun at any one."

I muttered, "I thought the safety was on."

Critter just glared at me.

Robert continued, "And you never, never put your finger on the trigger until--."

"I got it, kid," I shot out with anger at my own stupidity.

"Obviously you don't," Robert said, stepping forward as if to fight. Despite this being my fault, I was about ready to fight as well, simply driven by the anger at my stupidity and carelessness.

All of us stopped as Bryan, followed by Adam, stormed up to our group. I was ready for him to dump a torrent of insults at me. Instead Bryan went face to face with Critter. Their noses were about an inch apart.

Critter said, "He accidentally pulled the trigger."

"No kidding!" Bryan raged through clenched teeth, "Who gave that idiot the gun?"

"I asked Critter if he could show me—" I started to say.

"Shut up," Bryan said without looking at me. "Who gave him the gun?" he asked Critter again.

"I did," Critter said firmly. "We are in a literal zombie apocalypse. He needs to learn."

Bryan grabbed Critter's collar and Critter reared his fist back ready to strike like a cobra, but before Bryan could yell at Critter and a fight break out, Adam stepped between them. I don't think that I could have pushed them apart with all my strength, but somehow he had more power than Moses parting the Red Sea. He didn't use force. He just commanded respect and naturally received it. Somehow he just gently but firmly insinuated himself between them and they parted.

A crowd gathered around us.

Adam said calmly, "Brothers. Brothers. Yes, he needs to learn to shoot and it looks like he will learn a lot sooner than intended, a whole hell of a lot sooner. With the distance of that horde, we have less than six hours for the main group of eaters to get here if our calculations are correct. In the meantime we have a ton of work to do. Fighting amongst ourselves is not one of our jobs. First of all, we need to work on the wall defense. We need to make a lot of big stakes."

Scott started to open his mouth.

However, Adam snapped his fingers and said, "Scott, if this has anything to do with large stakes and your damned pecker, shut it!" Adam's eyes flared like dragon's fire for a split second and then went back to his usual calm.

Scott raised a finger as if he was going to offer a rebuttal, then closed his mouth and shrugged like Adam's call was correct.

Adam then looked at Bryan, "You are in charge of the wall. Round up the people you need and get to work immediately."

"You got it," said Bryan. He gave Critter one last dirty look and then took off to fulfill his mission.

Then Adam turned his eyes to Critter and me. "You two are going to run and meet the horde head on. Try to divert them a different way if possible, get a tree or boulder to block their path or kill as many and slow them as much as you can. The slower the zombies advance, the better our wall will be. Your job is to buy us any time that you can."

"I'll go with you," Scott volunteered.

Adam said, "You're too old and fat." Before Robert could volunteer, Adam said, "and I have seen the way you've been limping. Your knee is not ready to go on a long trek."

"I'll go!" I heard a man behind us volunteer

I looked and saw Tomas with his arm raised. He was the man who defended me when Bryan first brought me into the village. He was energized and ready to do what was necessary.

"Get your sword, Eric," Critter ordered.

For some reason, I stayed rooted to the ground until Tomas yelled at me, "Let's go! You caused this, now help fix it."

I rushed to pick up my short sword and sprinted back as Tomas and Critter started to jog out of the camp.

Critter said over his shoulder to Tomas, "No time for grudges. We have our ville to save."

I was actually glad to accompany these two on the venture just to get out of the camp. People cast the evil eye upon me as I ran past. Some seemed to want my blood more than the blood of the zombies.

We had barely gotten out of the circle of tents and I was already out of breath. I barely coughed out my question, "How far are we going, and what are we doing when we get there?"

"Save your breath! We'll know when we get there," Tomas snapped.

Other than the crunch of the leaves beneath our boots and the rasp of my breath, we ran in silence. I wasn't as sure footed as Critter and Tomas, so I was constantly stumbling and falling over roots and loose rocks. Twice they scolded me when I loudly cursed my clumsy misfortune.

I followed the two men at a quick jog. We took a trail that followed the small creek that went through the ville. It was a continuous downhill run. Every few hundred feet I would see a breathtaking waterfall. Were I not exhausted, humiliated by my mistake, and terrified of what we might run into ahead, I would have loved to have enjoyed and photographed each of the cascades. The journalist in me did make a mental note to follow this trail in a more peaceful time, if I survived, of course.

After a mile or so, we were deep in a hollow. It was a place that the sun rarely reached because of its narrow depth. The overcast was grey with heavy clouds that looked as if they wished to unload their burdens of rain upon us at any moment. These two factors made the day look like twilight even though that was about an hour or more away.

Critter and Tomas suddenly slowed to a fast walk. I was about to collapse to the ground, thinking we were taking a break. However, they drew their swords with a deadly hiss of the blade against the scabbard and started charging ahead. I gasped as up ahead, I saw five of those eaters, as Adam called the zombies, and a few more lumbering behind the main group.

Critter's and Tomas' swords were like lightning as they impacted the group of zombies. It was my job to describe what I saw, but I couldn't see specific techniques. As their swords slashed, the bodies of the zombies crashed to the ground as if they were indeed struck by lightning. In a literal flash of the blade, the enemy was vanquished.

Critter looked to Tomas and said, "Stop," before he could kill the last ones.

My companions stopped and turned to look at me. I thought they were going to dish out some violence on me for my mistake. I wondered if they had led me here to kill me far away from any witnesses.

"Why isn't your sword drawn?" Critter demanded.

"We were under attack." Tomas said in a tone that accused me of treason.

"What?" I asked. I quit walking. I felt suddenly paralyzed with fear as they walked up to me with their swords up, still dripping with the black zombie goo.

"Draw your weapon," Critter demanded as they walked towards me, weapons at their side but clenched in their hands with the tips pointed at me.

"I don't want to fight you guys," I pleaded.

They looked disgusted.

"Draw or you will have to fight us," Tomas threatened.

I hesitantly drew my sword. As the two men walked toward me, they stepped away from each other as if to surround me. I clenched my sword with two hands and held it before me and pointed up like I remembered seeing on a Star Wars poster.

Critter walked up to me, his sword still at his side.

"Oh my God!" I exclaimed.

Behind Critter and Tomas, I watched two zombies lurch towards us. Those things had deteriorated further than the original five and were moving much slower. I could see their teeth where their cheeks and lips had disintegrated.

"These two are yours," Critter said. "Step forward like a man and take care of business."

Critter grabbed the fabric of my coat behind the shoulder and gently, but firmly, propelled me forward to the rotters.

"Breathe," he said. "I'm right beside you, but if you don't kill them, I will let them kill you."

I blew out the pent up breath that I didn't realize that I had caught. I was panting and even more out of breath than I had been from the run.

The first zombie shambled into a ten foot radius of me and continued its approach. The other was eight feet behind him. I held the sword in front. Deep inside, I hoped they would see the threat and back up.

"Slash, now," Critter calmly instructed as if teaching me to slice a plastic bottle in a safe dojo setting. This was nothing to him.

I hacked at the first one's outstretched hand. The monster howled in an inhuman emotion. I panicked as my sword was stuck in its arm bone. It howled again and I could smell the rotten contents of its fetid lungs.

"Slice," Critter yelled with a sense of urgency. He pulled my arm down causing the sword to release.

"Go for the throat," he commanded. There was no calm in his voice now. The creature was upon us. I brought the sword across the neck and the head spun and flew from the lifeless body and crashed into a tree.

As I watched the body drop, Critter screamed, "Get the next one or you die! No! You will not die! You will become a walking rotting corpse like them! I will not save you!" He shoved me forward.

As I raised the blade, I realized the last zombie was a woman. I hesitated with the blade above my head as I still stumbled toward it from the push.

Critter screamed in my ear, "Later, we can debate chivalry vs. feminism at the campfire. Kill this bitch or you will die."

He pushed me forward again into the zombie's arm reach. With a savage gleam in her eyes and a roar from her ragged remaining lips, the thing suddenly and surprisingly lunged with inhuman speed at the sight of its meal. It was either slash her or be devoured. I slashed. The cut sliced through the left side of her neck and wedged in the right ribcage. Her body paralyzed, it almost sank to the ground. However my sword held her body up. Her teeth clicked viciously at me and her right arm grasped.

"Slice her head. End it!" one of my companions commanded.

I yanked the blade back and sliced through her skull. She was dead and I watched the psychotic gleam leave her eyes like electricity leaving the bulb of an old fashioned light.

I would have cursed if I had any breath.

"Good job," said Critter. "I knew you had it in you."

"Yeah man," agreed Tomas.

I leaned over with my hands on my knees. I almost retched. The exertion, nerves and the stench of the zombie goo was almost too much.

"I about froze," I gasped.

Critter chuckled. He was calm now as he said, "We all freeze the first time. I would have been there if you goofed up. I may not be there next time. Now stand upright and hold your head up like a man. You are an official zombie slayer now," he said seriously, but with a slight smile of pride.

I did stand taller. I felt that feeling of power and brotherhood. When Critter patted my shoulder, I spontaneously hugged him. He wasn't a hugger. He put the side of his hips to me and patted me on the back.

I turned to Tomas, who shook his head and said, "We are nowhere near done. We have to save a village yet. There are thousands behind these, I assure you."

He still blames and hates me, I thought with both guilt and resentment.

"Let's go," said Critter.

I nodded and turned my body so that the hidden cameras could get a good picture of the zombies. Then I followed.

We jogged another few hundred yards and already I was starting to lag behind. They left the ravine formed by the creek and ran up a little used trail that followed a steep hill. Shortly after that, my companions stopped. I sprinted the last few feet in hopes that they wouldn't notice how far I had been lagging.

However, they had no eyes for me, only for what was ahead.

"Oh crap," Critter said with pure dread.

I caught up and asked, "What?"

They stood on a precipice. I inched closer to the overlook and swore as well. About a half mile away and down about five hundred yards in elevation, it looked like the crowd at a rock concert. The zombies were packed into an open space in a canyon. There was an unnatural way the mass moved. It was as if even their bones knew that they weren't supposed to be moving, but they were moving anyway, and in our direction. There were thousands of them.

Tomas and I swore.

Critter said, "I don't think it's that bad. Halfway between us and them there is a ravine. If we get there first, we can block the way here and funnel them into the ravine."

"How?" demanded Tomas.

"We'll chop down some trees, use rocks. We'll even lead them, if necessary. It doesn't matter. We'll think of something. Hell, maybe we'll kill enough to stack the bodies up like a wall." I thought he was joking about the last part.

"We'll just have to deal with them later. Eventually they'll go over the hill and get to the village," Tomas griped.

"Then we'll either move camp before or attack them when we are more prepared. Either way it will buy us time."

"But—" Tomas started to protest irritably.

"Quit hoping we fail so you can maintain your hatred for Eric." Critter growled. "We will succeed. We must. Let's go, quickly."

"What about him?" Tomas asked.

"I can keep up." I said between panting breaths. I was leaning over with my hands on my knees to support my body's weight.

Critter clenched his lips and made a snap decision, "Go back down to the creek at the bottom of this trail, and stay there," he ordered. "If we're not back by dark, follow along this creek back to the village without us."

"They'll kill me if I show back by myself," I said.

Tomas snorted with derision. He didn't care what happened to me. I had committed a cardinal sin in his eyes.

Critter pointed at my face with all five fingers extended at me and said, "You will just slow our work down. Just walk back down to the creek and wait. No arguments."

That settled it. They took off at twice the speed they were jogging before. They practically flew straight down the hill, leaping with gravity over rocks and roots. I couldn't have kept up anyway, and slowed to a walk until I reached the creek.

For a moment I felt good about getting a break. As they disappeared and I caught my wind, I felt guilty for slowing them down, but the longer I looked at the trail that had swallowed them, the more alone I felt, and the more the terror seeped back inside of me.

I stepped off of the trail. There was a small cove that reminded me of a mini amphitheater made of granite that circled the area in which I stood. It was about thirty feet across. I imagined a drama shown in ancient Greece playing there. A small waterfall fell into the amphitheater. I backed into the clearing and sat on a stone. It seemed almost as dark as night when the drizzle began to fall from the sky. However, there was still another quarter hour or so until full dark.

A few moments passed and my breathing returned to normal. I listened to the falling precipitation that competed with the sound of the small waterfall. I suddenly realized my feet were soaked. I looked down and saw my boots were in a few inches of water. The water that flowed into the amphitheater spread out forming a small swampy area. I had a feeling of déjà vu. Something about the dark, swampy water and the natural amphitheater caused a tremor of horror to rip through me as I could feel the spongey, loamy soil beneath my boots.

It was weird. I think I somehow sensed them before I could see, hear, or smell them. It was a feeling. A mortal terror that welled up in my chest. I was looking at the ground between my feet. I suddenly looked up knowing that I would see them before me. I was in that amphitheater-like area where I met Abigail in my dream.

Four cloaked and hooded figures in black stood before me as if they had appeared from nowhere. I caught my breath and with a gasp, I couldn't move, whether by their power or my terror, I did not know.

These were not zombies. In the darkness in the yawning maw of their cloaks, their faces almost glowed a sickly pale. A malevolent intelligence burned in their eyes behind the recess of their hoods. A cruel mirth slashed their lips. These were the same cloaked and hooded figures I had seen in the video observing the zombies attack.

A woman's cackle emitted from one of the hoods, "Are you lost, human?"

I stood speechless at the way she called me human.

"Maybe he's deaf." A male voice suggested when I didn't answer. Then he laughed and said, "Or maybe he just can't hear."

"Or dumb," another woman laughed. It was a throaty sensual purr. I gaped at her. She was the vampire woman in my dream.

As one, they all lowered their hoods as if knowing the effect of pure terror that it would inspire. I couldn't draw my sword. My only instinct was to back up. I pushed back with my heels and fell off of a rock. It was only a few inches, but I couldn't function. On the ground, I kept pushing back, scooting on my butt. My pants were suddenly thoroughly soaked from the water. I backed into the rock wall of the amphitheater. If one was there, I would have squeezed into a six inch wide rabbit hole strictly powered by terror.

I scrambled to my feet.

One of them, an older, middle aged male stepped forward and I reached for my sword.

"There is no need for that, young man," he said.

The calmness of his voice somehow convinced me. I hesitated, hand still on the handle of the sword. He placed his hand on mine, keeping it still. It was the coldest human hand that ever touched me. It felt below freezing.

"Relax. We just want to talk to you," he said.

"Yes. Talk is all we want, human," the older female vampire chuckled softly.

I looked at her. At one point she may have struck me as attractive. It wasn't her age but rather that she looked like evil itself. I looked at her dark eyes and pale skin. I couldn't tell if the paleness was natural or due to make-up. There was an air of theatrics with them. I hesitate to say they struck me as Goths or the vampire wannabe fad. I don't know how to describe it. There was some acting going on, but the actual deviltry was also palpable.

I released my sword handle, and the male figure let go of my hand.

"Why do you call me human as if you're not?" I asked.

The young woman said, "We are not. We are beyond. We are better. We are what you dream to be. I am Abigail."

"I know," I said without thinking.

The man stepped back, and Abigail stepped forward. "We just want to talk."

Her eyes were full of all kinds of suggestive seductions. There was a stirring in me for all the promises that both a good and a bad girl could deliver. Yes, it was a cheesy thought in such a dire situation, but I felt that I was also truly under their spell at that moment.

"Talk about what?" I asked.

"Your tribe is in trouble," the older woman said. I looked at her. She had the same seductive power as the younger woman. Maybe more so with the promise of experience.

"Let us help you," the younger woman purred.

"Or we can hurt you more," the youngest male spoke up.

"Lucius!" scolded the older man in a quiet but harsh whisper, but none of their eyes left me. They had the look of four wolves who had cornered a rabbit.

I looked at each of them. Each of them stared with that promise that anything was possible. It was a promise of not just sexual delights, but power, riches, deep undreamed of dreams. Immortality? Everything was in my grasp if I just talked to them. It was all in their eyes—I don't know how else to explain it. It was there in their stare.

But there had to be a string.

"What do you want?" I asked.

In the most pleasant voice imaginable the older man said, "Give just a little of your blood."

I jumped back into the wall and almost fell again. I fought to stay on my feet. I suddenly found my sword in my hands held in front of me. The hilt at my waist. My blade pointed at their eyes. I made a point to aim the tip at each of their faces. I was no rabbit.

"There's no need for that." Abigail said with compassion. "Giving over a little of your blood won't kill you, and you will truly live afterwards."

"More than you could imagine," assured Lucius.

I believed them. I lowered my sword slightly and Lucius charged. I slashed across his chest. It sliced deep against his rib cage. I could feel each rib bump like a xylophone. I stepped to the side with the slash. I had learned to do this in prior martial classes, but this was the first time it came naturally. I backed into a corner with a sword pointing at them.

The vamps, including Lucius, drew their swords. All of their swords were at least a foot longer than mine. I cursed Bryan and the short Wakizashi. The blades gleamed despite the gloom. They had intricate designs of dragons and lore. They looked fantastical. Like something a harmless geek would buy simply because it looked cool, but again I could sense the deadliness of their sleek designs.

The vampires smiled. This was a game to the death. A game I did not want to lose. A game that I wasn't sure I could win.

I held my sword with my left hand, still pointed at them. I slapped myself in the face as hard as I could with my right hand. My brain, my soul did not feel like my own.

Abigail dropped her sword to her side and looked at me with her lips pursed. Her lips didn't move, but I heard deep inside my head. "You fear that tribe you live with. You fear the home you can't go to. You fear your enemies. You fear your friends. You fear us. You fear death. You even fear to live. We can take your fear. You can live blissfully with us." I heard them all speaking the last line at once as if through clouds. I closed my eyes to clear my head.

I heard Abigail whisper, "You can live blissfully with me," in my ear.

I opened my eyes, turned my head, and saw her crimson lips inches from me. How did she close the distance? I smelled her intoxicating natural perfume and the smell of earth with a negligible hint of the soil decay of the forest. Her body seemed to move as if floating and gently stirred by the faintest of breezes.

I shook the tantalizing hypnotic effect away and looked her fully in the eyes. I realized that she communicated telepathically. Somehow they had a spell over me that I had just accepted. Their telepathy also woke something in my brain that felt as if it had simply been in slumber. I almost felt as if my mind physically re-organized to open communication with her.

She stopped her hypnotic movements and beheld me with curiosity. Again I heard deep in my head as if she spoke aloud, "You can hear every word, can't you? Most can only sense emotions behind the words."

Telepathically, I said, "Yes," I looked at the other vampires and then told her telepathically, "I can hear the doubts of your friends right now. They don't think that you will kill me. They suspect you are a traitor."

I looked at her as I heard her mind say, "Yes. You are an anomaly like me. They woke up the same latent abilities, but other vamps can just sense emotions, not full words like you and me. The vampire virus was simply an experiment to give us psionic abilities. Instead it turned us into these freaks. You are supposed to be my first kill, but I can't."

"Abigail! Is there a problem?" The older man demanded aloud. I somehow knew that his name was Richard and that he was the leader of this clan.

She said out loud, "He has our abilities and greater." She looked at me and I heard her voice in my head, "I can not do this to you." I saw abject terror in her eyes.

"Kill him," shouted Lucius..

"No," Abigail shouted.

I looked at Richard. He did something with his eyes and I felt like a black cloth sack had been thrown over my head.

I closed my eyes for a moment. I heard the high pitched shriek of demonic animals. I saw Lucius thrown across the small amphitheater and smashed into the granite wall. I saw Abigail looking into my eyes. I saw the hint of new fear in her and she collapsed to the ground as a black leather fist crashed into her skull. I looked, expecting to see Critter or Tomas, but what I saw brought a new terror to my soul.

"Thanks," I mumbled numbly to my rescuer.

The hulking, skull faced man glared down at me from his towering height. A deep gravelly inhuman voice growled at them. "Lucius, Richard, Emma, Abigail! Stay away from this fool! He is mine!"

"Yes Specter," the vamps said as a chorus. Except for Abigail, who I took for dead with a crushed skull and a broken neck. I didn't think anyone could survive that savage blow to the temple.

I said the name of my rescuer, "Specter?"

He swung at me with his arm, but he struck me with an open back hand. He continued to slap me brutally back and forth until I fell to the ground next to the motionless Abigail.

I looked up at him and could see the skull face was a kind of mask. That did not relieve my terror. I stared speechless at the monster.

He pointed a finger clad in black leather. There was leather and spikes on his wrist. Not the somewhat harmless spikes usually seen on punks. These spikes looked razor sharp and regularly honed. The brutal slaps he gave me could have been deadly or at least disfiguring had he used the spikes. I guess that he didn't want me dead just yet, but it did not allay my fears at all.

Pointing at me he said in his deep, inhuman voice. "You are a dead man. But you will not die until I give the word. Do you understand?"

"Yes sir," I stammered.

"Vamps?" the Specter called.

"Yes Specter," sang the chorus sans Abigail.

"Is Abigail dead?" I interrupted. Despite my fear and understanding of what The Specter had probably saved me from, I couldn't help but feel bad if she had to die. My brain felt like it was made of Styrofoam. I think I was still under a spell of sorts.

He slowly turned his head towards me. A maniacal humor gleamed beneath the brows. A deep growl emitted from his mouth that I took to be something that resembled a laugh.

"Specter. The humans return," said Richard in a tone like a college professor.

"I know. Do they scare you?" the Specter asked the vamps.

There was no answer.

The Specter answered his question, "Nothing scares The Specter. Remember that."

The Specter glared at them.

The vamps answered in chorus, "Yes Specter."

"Leave," the Specter ordered.

"What of Abigail?" Lucias asked.

"Go!" The Specter ordered with a booming voice. "Leave her to the humans."

The Vamps disappeared in the dark. I realized that the sun had long ago set. I could barely see anything other than Abigail's pale lifeless face and the white of The Specter's skull mask in the gloom of the drizzling rain and depth of the hollow. He nodded once to me. Then springing like a cheetah, he leaped upon a stone that was at my head's height. I noted that he was either supernatural or a hell of an athlete. He leapt again to a higher stone and slunk off into the dark, hunched over in a commando crouch. Before he left my sight, I saw the assault rifle strapped to his shoulder. It was something like an M-16 with some hi-tech scope and other gear. He also had a ubiquitous sword.

I bent to pick up my sword that had fallen forgotten from my fingers earlier. As I stood with my sword at the ready, two dark figures entered the amphitheater with their swords drawn and bloody.

They stopped as they saw my sword pointed at them. There stood Critter and Tomas.

I lowered my sword.

They looked at Abigail's body.

"Good for you," said Tomas. "Your first zombie by yourself."

Critter kicked her lifeless body over. "What the hell!" he exclaimed as his pistol replaced the sword in his hand. Guns were only used in the most dire of situations. The fact that Abigail was dead at his feet made it clear that the vampires were not taken lightly at all.

"What?" asked Tomas.

"That's not a zombie," Critter said.

"A person?" asked Tomas.

"A vamp!" Critter said as he squatted down to examine Abigail. He was calm, but on red alert. He poked the limp body and turned her head with the gun's barrel.

"Baloney!" exclaimed Tomas.

"Are they rare?" I asked.

"You're the first vamp slayer I know of," Critter chuckled but nervously looked around. "They don't hang out by themselves or abandon their own from what I've heard."

"Stab her through the heart to make sure," said Tomas.

Critter holstered his pistol and lifted his blade, but I pushed him aside as he started to impale her.

"She's dead," I claimed. "I already stabbed her heart."

I stepped over her body protectively. For some reason, disfiguring and mutilating the dead felt like a line I could not cross. I told myself I may have to kill another person to live, but mutilation seemed like the first step to losing my humanity even if it was a zombie or vampire. They were once human.

Critter glared at me. "Were you bit by her?"

"Of course not!" My blood went cold. I didn't know what happened in that moment where everything became cloudy. I didn't even know how long that moment when I closed my eyes lasted. My hand instinctively went to my throat. I felt something on my neck.

Critter came up and shined his headlamp over me to inspect for any vamp or zombie violations and poked and slapped me all over to see if I had a wound that would cause me to cry out in pain when prodded.

"Is he bit?" Tomas asked with his sword raised to strike me down at the slightest head nod from Critter.

"He's clean from what I can see."

I sighed in relief, but put on an angry act. "I told you," I said as I pushed him back for roughly searching me.

The pain in my neck was gone. I suspected it was probably psychosomatic. I remembered as a kid, we'd get teased in school if we were found to have head lice. So every time we'd get inspected, my scalp would suddenly itch from pure nervous suggestion.

"Damn, Eric's grown some cojones," said Tomas.

I didn't feel brave. Just sad and angry. I had seen enough death.

"No, I'm not brave." I said. "We have a village to protect. Let's go."

"Good idea," said Critter. I saw Critter's mouth open in surprise. He pointed at the ground. "The Specter was here," he said. "The boot print."

I looked and couldn't see the boot print, even as I turned on my headlamp. Critter's skills at tracking were indeed legendary.

"You know him, The Specter?" I asked. "We talked about him, but..."

"We're not drinking buddies," he joked, "but I've trailed him. He mostly haunts the Low Boys."

I said. "I caught a glimpse of him. He looked scary."

Critter snorted, "He doesn't scare me."

"He looked somewhat supernatural," I said.

Critter laughed, pointing at the ground and drawled, "Not unless ghosts leave footprints from wearing combat boots."

"Too many monsters out tonight, let's get back to camp," Tomas said with grim resolve.

As we turned to go, Tomas and Critter led the way. I took one last look at Abigail as she lay at the base of the rock. I almost screamed. Her eyes were opened and full of life, looking straight inside of me. Her face was still, but her eyes opened with a spark of vital energy. She was staring at me from the ground. It was the same look she gave me in my dream when she warned me.

Critter stopped and looked at me, "What?"

"Nothing."

I looked again and Abigail's eyes were closed.

Critter and Tomas looked at each other, shrugged and started on their way back home. I followed.

I turned back to look at Abigail one last time. She now stood, looking at me with a perplexing gaze. For some reason,

I expected that. We held eye contact and it was one of those brief looks between two people who know that an unknown providence and destiny bonds them. That feeling of destiny would later prove frightfully correct. She smiled at me, stepped back, and disappeared into the gloom. I walked for a moment confused with my thoughts. It all had been dream-like, but it was all real.

The spell suddenly broke. I finally felt like myself. It then felt like ice water was poured down my back as the full weight of it hit me. I really should have killed her while she was at our feet, I thought. Despite my exhaustion, I had no problem keeping up with my companions on my way back to the village. No amount of exhaustion would cause me to be alone this dark night, I thought as I heard the howls of the undead in the forest around me.

| 16 |

However, we didn't run straight back to the village. Several times we stopped and waited for some of the stronger, faster zombies to catch us. Each time we'd cut them down and then retreat. We'd stop and make another stand and cut more down. Occasionally, we'd cut down a tree or use boulders to block a narrow part of the trail to stall or divert the mass movement up another trail, but all our efforts were only temporary. It was like trying to stop the tide from coming in by using a wall made of sand.

Other times we'd run into zombies who were ahead of us already. I suspected these came down from the mountains above. Whether before us or behind us, we smote as many as we could.

All I remember from the combat that night were glimpses of rotted and malformed features as my headlamp flickered on the screaming zombies as I slashed at them with my sword. I lost count after I killed eleven of them. They came from everywhere. It seemed even the branches of trees were striking at us in the confusion. My memory is like a strobe light from the three of our headlamps constantly moving checking all around us in the dark forest. Occasionally Critter's or Tomas's light would splash across my eyes blinding me for a terrifying moment. They cursed at me when I blinded them. I learned to keep the light lower.

Then the nightmare happened. I sliced through a zombie's neck and its arm knocked the headlamp off my head, plunging my world into darkness. I picked up the darkened headlamp but the batteries were missing, hidden in the fallen leaves and stones of the forest floor. I called for my companions to shine a light, but they had moved ahead. I scrambled to catch up, hacking at any noise that stood or walked between me and them.

One by one, Critter's and Tomas's lamps went out due to the continued violence of our encounters. For thirty minutes we made our way in pitch black, mostly through the feel of the steady rise of the trail. Occasionally we'd engage in combat mostly by striking at anything that growled or screeched in the distorted manner produced by the flesh of a decaying throat.

Every few seconds my companions and I would hiss at each other in harsh stifled tones to be sure we didn't accidentally slice each other. There was a lot of swearing along with reassurances,

"I'm here."
"Beside you."
"Is that you, brother?"
"Yeah."

"Watch it."

"What's that?"

With the swords covered in infectious goo, we feared even the slightest accidental prick would turn us into one of them.

After what seemed like an eternity, I saw a light ahead. It looked like the flickering fires of hell. I stared ahead seeing the distant quivering reddish glare cause the shadows of the trees to dance. I expected something terrible, hideously supernatural, but instead, as we drew near, I realized that it was the safety of the torches of the village. Tomas, Critter and I stumbled up to the barriers.

There were sliced up and decapitated zombie bodies laying all over the ground. These must have come from over the mountain I guessed.

The flickering shadows of armed men and sharpened stakes pointing at me will always be burned in my memory. I saw a man raise a spear to throw, when Critter urgently yelled, "It's us."

"Cross the barrier, slowly," said Bryan.

We crossed and Bryan greeted us with joy. "I am so glad to see you guys. We've been getting attacked randomly and feared you were surrounded."

"We were surrounded," said Critter with a casual shrug as if it was just another day at the office.

Bryan was about to give Critter a spontaneous hug, but he abruptly stepped back.

"You guys need to wash up. You might get infected. Tomorrow you three will be on quarantine watch in case you're already infected just from your contact," Bryan said.

I looked at Tomas and Critter. They were covered in the zombie goo. I looked at my arms that were covered in that crap as well. I sniffed my arms and regretted it instantly as I began to retch.

They ignored me. This was a common reaction even with the most seasoned warriors. The body wanted nothing to do with the zombie's toxic nature.

Critter ruefully shook his head. "The entire ville is going to have to watch everyone for possible infection after tonight."

"What's the status?" Bryan asked.

"We're screwed boss. I mean, I think we'll pull through, some of us at least," Critter added as he cast a doubtful glance at me, "but, no one will get any sleep tonight."

"Is that an exaggeration?" asked Bryan.

"I think he is overly optimistic if he thinks our only problem is disturbed sleeping patterns," Tomas opined.

Critter answered Bryan, "Does this look like a fricking exaggeration?" he motioned to the muck on his body. I then saw that his katana was missing the top half of its blade. It must have shattered in the dark combat, but despite the broken sword he had valiantly battled on.

"I am sorry, my friend," said Bryan. "Report what you saw."

"Thousands. Maybe tens of thousands."

"Could you divert them," Bryan asked.

"We did divert some thousands or so, but they're headed up Dark Cove and may surround us in a day or so if they follow the oak knob trail."

Bryan sighed, "Wash up. We'll need you back here."

"You got it," said Critter.

I practically ran to the creek to wash off the filth.

"Stop!" roared Bryan.

I stopped at the bank and looked at him.

Critter pointed back to where we came from, the other side of the barrier. "Downstream. This part of the creek is where we drink, and trust me; we'll need plenty of fresh, clean water to rehydrate during the coming combat."

With new flashlights and torches, we walked forward, stripped off our clothes, and washed that nasty stuff off with soap and water. The temperature was about 50 F but the cold water actually felt good after the heat of the running battle. We then rubbed some homemade hand sanitizer over our bodies. I found out later they had taken gallons of denatured alcohol looted from hardware stores in ravaged cities and mixed it with antiseptic herbs such as the tannic acid from the acorns, garlic, and mixed it. It was applied liberally over anyone or anything that even came within sight of a zombie. The antiseptic didn't smell great, but it smelled better than zombie goo.

Adam looked us over for bites and then someone gave us fresh clothes, and I quickly got dressed as the night's chill began to seep back into my bones.

When I started to go back to the frontlines, Critter stopped me. "In case you got some of that zombie crap in your mouth, you need to disinfect your insides."

I looked at him in terror and started to deny any zombie goo touching my lips. I still feared that they would slay me if they had any suspicion of me being infected.

He winked and handed me a bottle of bourbon whiskey. I was about to refuse, remembering my vow to stop drinking, but instead I smiled and chugged a shot. I winced as the fiery liquid burned its way down to my belly. I took another drink from the bottle. When I tried for a third drink, Critter took it from me and said with a grim chuckle, "Easy. This is for calming the nerves, not numbing them. You'll need all your faculties. In fact, we're going to need every man including you to bring his "A" game tonight."

I nodded and said, "I was with you when we saw that horde remember."

The three of us went back on our side of the line. I learned that the barrier was set up three hundred meters in front of the village in a narrow part of the cove. The tents were abandoned and the young children and those who were unable to fight were set up on a steep part on the hill above. A few warriors would be stationed with the one pair of night vision goggles as a last ditch defense for those who couldn't defend themselves.

As this was being explained to me Anna, Bryan's wife, showed up on the lines.

"What are you doing here?" Bryan demanded.

"I thought you might need help on the wall," she said, gripping her sword, ready for a fight.

"I need you back with the kids in case we fail," Bryan demanded.

Anna stood arms akimbo and shot right back, "Would you stay put if your mate was facing probable death? It's my village too."

Bryan just looked at her as if afraid to say something. He finally said, "I'm in charge of defense and I am ordering you to protect the children. That's a more important job than protecting empty tents, which is basically what we're doing on this line."

She stood her ground and pointed at me, "Why is he here? I'm better with the sword than he is."

Bryan snorted, "Would you prefer that Eric go back and defend our children."

She shook her head and glared at him for a moment as if searching for a retort and finally settled on, "It's because I'm a woman."

Bryan hesitated for a moment. "Don't give me that! We do have women on the line tonight."

As Bryan paused, a worried look crossed his face, and Adam stepped forward seemingly out of nowhere. His tone was gentle, but his eye contact with Anna was firm as if he meant every word.

"You are alive right now strictly because you are a woman," Adam said. "If a man, such as Critter or Eric, disobeyed a direct order during a crisis like this, they would immediately be shot on my orders. If you still demand equality, I can arrange that."

He stared at her until she turned around and went back without another word.

Bryan placed his head in his hand and sighed.

Adam said sagely, "Shake it off and do your job. She's only worried about you and will hug you in the morning."

Critter said, "Hey Bryan, don't go knocking Eric's skill as a swordsman."

"Why is that?" asked Bryan.

"He slayed a vampire," Critter bragged on me as he slapped my back.

All eyes were upon me, and I didn't like it.

Scott laughed, "A regular Buffy, only not so cute to look at. We should get you a blonde wig and a stake."

Everyone looked impressed except Bryan. He said, "No one in our tribe has killed one or gotten close and lived. How did this happen?"

I felt like I was giving a public speech and the spotlight was blinding me. "It tried to bite my neck and I stabbed its heart, and slashed it, like you taught me."

Bryan nodded. "They're not known for approaching groups of people. They prey on the solitary. Is that what you saw, Critter, Tomas?"

Critter explained, "We had to move faster than he could move. He was alone for maybe a half hour at the most."

Bryan turned and faced Critter with his full fury, "You disobeyed a direct protocol. No one is to be left alone outside the ville, especially that guy."

Critter stepped up holding eye contact inches from Bryan's face. "Excuse me for making a command decision in the field to save the fricking village. Sorry I didn't send a runner to ask your permission to wipe my ass. Tomas and I purchased some valuable time and killed some bad guys, I would do it again. Right Tomas?"

"We did what we had to do," said Tomas. "I would do the same if I was in charge."

Critter kept his full attention at Bryan. The firelight from the torches burned in his eyes as he challenged, "So you want to immediately shoot me like Adam threatened your wife?"

"Same with me," I said.

Tomas stepped forward as well.

"Stand down men. Critter did what needed to be done at the time," Adam said.

Bryan sighed and looked at Critter. "I didn't mean to second guess you out there. I just have a lot of worries in my mind. My family--"

"At least you have a family to worry about," Critter shot back.

"Brothers," Adam said. "We're all under a lot of stress. Critter, you did well out there, but Bryan is apologizing and you're still trying to keep the fight alive. We have worse enemies than each other this evening."

"He's right, man. I just had a lot of crap on my mind as well," Critter said, extending a hand.

Bryan shook it and gave Critter a hug with his free hand. "Let's kick some ass, old friend."

"You got it, man," Critter replied with a half hug that was more of a slap on the back.

"I don't mean to butt in, but what do you need me to do?" I asked.

Bryan stepped forward and looked me over exactly as Critter had done to see if I had been bitten.

"Adam and Critter already checked me," I assured him.

He nodded, "I'm sure, but redundancy has saved us in the past." He finally looked satisfied with his quick inspection.

I repeated my inquiry, "What do you need me to do?"

I saw a hint of concern behind his otherwise stoic features. "Right now you need to sit under that tree and rest. Your stomach may be churning, but you also need to eat."

I felt insulted. "I can fight," I said.

"I know, and trust me, you will," said Bryan.

"Yeah," Critter said. "He probably killed thirty of them along with the vamp."

Bryan nodded, "Not bad for your first day on the job, but thirty is nothing compared to the thousands we will face in an hour or so."

I saw the weight of his responsibilities weighing on him. Although Bryan hadn't been on the run, he actually looked more exhausted than I did. I swallowed any argument and walked to the big poplar tree and sat under it. There was a tarp tied above. It had stopped drizzling, but the tarp had kept the leaves dry. I sat down and marveled how I considered dry leaves to be a luxury that I actually cherished in that briefest of moments before the great battle.

My resting spot was ten feet above the battle zone. I let my body cameras film the area. I studied their strategy. They picked a spot where the cove had narrowed to about thirty meters across with steep hillsides on either side that acted like a wall. The village had set up stakes that were planted into the ground at forty-five degree angles so that a charging combatant would stab himself with his momentum. There were five layers of these stake barriers.

A person in his right mind could easily navigate the stakes. The zombies had a minimal amount of mind, but they had the numbers that would push them from behind. It reminded me of the final stand at Helm's Deep. Only this wall was not to stop them, only to slow. It was only sheer manpower and sharpened, swinging steel that would stop them.

There were a few men and women standing guard in front of the barrier to cut down the sporadic vanguard before the zombie typhoon hit. In front of the barrier they had already strategically piled up the zombie bodies to further slow them down or funnel them for strategic reasons. I watched a tribesman slice down a lone zombie ahead of the barriers. Another warrior, a red haired woman, helped the defender carry and toss the new body on a strategically placed pile of corpses.

The grim men and women on the line faced down the cove. It was all they could do for the moment--dreading the coming confrontation, but wishing to get through with it no matter the outcome.

I hadn't prayed in a while, but I prayed that night. I stopped as sleepiness took my mind and my thoughts drifted to Jennifer, my girl back home, and then to the vampiress, Abigail. I closed my eyes and entered the darkness that she ruled.

| 17 |

I was shaken awake. I looked up in surprise at Critter standing over me. "They're here."

"Sorry, I didn't realize that I had fallen asleep," I apologized.

"Don't sweat it. You were asleep for less than an hour."

I stretched, lifting my arms to the starless, midnight sky and realized how sore I was from slicing and hacking with the sword, both in training and actual combat. I worried if I would be able to wield even my smaller blade. I twisted my crackling spine, and then I failed miserably when I tried to touch my toes. All of my muscles were as tight as a noose around a hanged man's neck.

"Let's go," said Critter.

All the men and women along the barrier went forward beyond the barriers to meet the zombies. We had lit many torches and placed them as far as the eye could see in the cove and the slopes on either side. It was eerie how the drizzly fog and smoke from the torches hung above the ground.

I heard a man swear about vampires. I looked up and saw six of them, including Richard, Emma and Lucius lit up by the flickering torches. For some reason, I worried about Abigail, who was absent.

"Do the vamps direct the zombies or are they just observing?" I asked Critter as I nervously looked up at them. The vamps were smiling with that superiority complex they displayed over humans. I was surprised that they didn't have popcorn, that is if they could eat regular food.

"They might be able to direct them or not. We know very little about them," he answered without taking his eyes off of them, "Mostly, we just go by legend. Pretty much like we did before the apocalypse."

"Were the legends based on actual truth?" I asked.

"Who knows?" he said with a shrug. He had a way of just accepting whatever was.

I saw Bryan string the short bow that he carried on his back and aim an arrow toward Richard. Despite being at the extreme range of the bow, I took satisfaction in seeing the vamp back up with the slightest apprehension. They did fear something besides The Specter, I reassured myself.

As Bryan brought the bow the full draw, Adam said loud but calm, "Stop Bryan. We may need every arrow for our zombie foes."

Bryan frowned and relaxed the draw of the bow. I saw Richard relax and then smile again.

"I hate those smug ass bastards," Bryan swore bitterly.

"I do too," said Adam. "I will keep an eye on them. If I see them do anything that may compromise us, I'll shoot them myself."

"Can vampires be killed with conventional weapons?" I asked, remembering how Abigail had survived the savage blow from The Specter.

Adam, Scott, Critter, and many others glared at me as Bryan said, "You, if anyone, should know."

"It was dark," I answered. They didn't buy it. Before they could question me further someone interrupted the moment.

"Sir!" someone yelled from the vanguard of our defense.

I looked and the army of the undead had finally arrived. These weren't stragglers. They were packed in with no more than a meter or two of space between them. They shuffled one right after another, endlessly. Bryan charged in front of everyone as he drew both katanas. He went into his windmill mode right into the middle of a mob swinging at anything in blade's reach, never missing a fatal blow. I felt my respect deepen for him. He was unstoppable. Heads literally flew from those heavy steel blades that he wielded like they were light aluminum. He could do with one hand what I could not do with two, and he was so good with both blades that I could never tell if he was right or left handed.

Everyone around me charged, screaming war cries at decibels enough to attempt to hide their fear. They plowed into the thick of the mass. I wondered why we didn't just wait behind the safety of the barriers, but I didn't have time to ask. I just fought as I charged with my mates, screaming at the top of my lungs. Each of our individual war cries rose in a mixed crescendo empowering the whole army.

With the new adrenalin, my sore muscles worked like new. I felt like a warrior, slashing and hacking at the undead around me. I caught sight of Scott wielding his Louisville Slugger baseball bat, whacking the hell out of one right after another like the Babe Ruth of the zombie apocalypse. Critter was also a blur in his movements. He wielded two swords as well. A big katana in his right and a smaller wakizashi in his left. His left hand wasn't as coordinated as his right. Critter mostly used the smaller sword for blocking, pushing, and close quarters fighting. However his right arm was flawless, maybe better than Bryan.

I told myself to stay close to the barricade, but I was quickly surrounded by those things. Every slice had to count. To miss or merely wound would mean they would close in enough to infect or devour me. I slew five and then I lost track. It was almost as if my spirit was watching me slay them from above. My body went automatic; my consciousness was only there for the ride.

Distantly I heard a booming voice yell, "Eric! Come back!"

I heard the command, but couldn't process the order. I was so intent on staying alive, slashing throats and stabbing through eye sockets and rancid hearts. Suddenly something yanked my shoulder. I tried to slash at it, but it placed a calm hand on my elbow immobilizing my arm from slashing. I tried to turn out of it fearing I'd be bitten.

"Follow me back! Keep fighting." Adam ordered as he released my arm.

I looked at him and saw my face reflected in his glasses from the glare of the flickering torchlight. I was fifty yards from the barrier in the middle of a thick part of the swarm.

"OK," I said breathlessly.

"You're doing great," Adam said. "Just keep your bearings."

I followed as he slashed a path back with the ease of a man half his age. The footing was rough. In many places there were two or more bodies piled up. The squishy, shifting feel beneath my boots would haunt my dreams for years, but at the moment my adrenaline-fueled blood burned that fear and distaste for the situation away like dry leaves in a bonfire.

I fought for a while when I again heard Adam's booming voice, "Behind the wall! Now!" he commanded everyone.

I fought my way back and stood next to the line of men and women. I caught my breath. We had done a great job defending the line and my companions could easily hack the zombies as they tried to scramble over the barriers that were made of both wooden stakes and freshly killed undead.

I looked at them and could sense hopelessness about them. I was confused. I thought we were really kicking ass.

"What's the matter," I asked.

"Look," said Scott. There was no humor in his eyes. It was like the light of life was removed from his soul.

In the firelight, I could see the zombies. It was no different than what we had been fighting. I could go another hour easily.

"What?" I asked.

"Look, dammit!" Scott said with an anger that I didn't think was possible for his goofy persona.

I looked to the farthest reaches of the firelight. At first I thought a dam of water had burst. It looked like the rapids of the Colorado River through the Grand Canyon, a roiling mass.

I swore as I finally realized what I was seeing.

The zombies were solidly packed together heading straight towards us. There was no space between them. It was an endless moving wall that extended as far as the eye could see. In the center of it, about a football field away, whirling like windmills in a hurricane were Bryan and Critter standing back to back.

I started to head back into the fray, but Scott grabbed my shoulder. "Stay."

"They need help." I said.

"Not from you," Scott said.

I was about to go off on him. Hadn't I proved my worth yet? A blood lust was burning in me.

Adam called out, "Bryan and Critter come back."

They were packed in so tight the two men could barely swing.

I ripped out of Scott's grasp. I heard him calling after me.

Adam said, "Let him go."

I charged swinging through the zombie vanguard and reached the shoulder to shoulder mass. I couldn't see Critter and Bryan. I could only see the turbulence they caused in the middle of the pack. I attacked at the wall of former humanity with my eye on their position.

I then saw Bryan jump up on a boulder and Critter followed. The head level of the zombies was up to their mid thighs. They were about thirty yards away. Despite my attacking, the zombie mass was pushing me back toward the barrier. It was hopeless. They were lost.

I saw Critter shout something at Bryan. Bryan nodded back and smirked resolutely at the dire fate.

Critter leaped into the mass and ran across the heads and shoulders like Jesus Christ himself walking on a stormy sea. Bryan followed, heading straight towards me.

Critter hurdled over my head and began fighting again by my side. Bryan stumbled behind him and fell into the mass, a few feet from me. I grabbed Bryan's shoulder and pulled him out. I stumbled, only to be righted by Scott.

"Get back or I'll bite you myself," Scott screamed in my ear.

I took him seriously and obeyed. We all fought our way back to the barrier just in time.

The shoulder to shoulder mass was at our first barrier. The defenders stood shoulder to shoulder as well. We had the higher ground and slashed at the mass beneath us as they tried to crawl over the stakes and slain zombies. The footing was treacherous. My boot was planted on a decapitated head. Its jaws continuously snapped, instinctively at the hard rubber sole.

We were stationed behind the first barrier of stakes, but were continuously pushed back. We could retreat together without giving up a space between us, but we must hold the final line of stakes. Once they were past that line, our cove widened and our line would break and the zombies would surround each individual.

If one warrior was pushed back the whole line retreated that equal distance to maintain the line to guard each other's flank and rear. Once our line was disrupted, we'd get surrounded and the village would be lost. Each fighter relied on his brother and sister on the line.

The battle raged late into the night and into the early and dark hours of the morning. We held our line, but we kept getting pushed back one foot, one inch, one meter at a time. We battled endlessly many times past the point of what we thought were our limits.

Eventually, we were pushed to the last barrier. We couldn't retreat any further. I also felt that I had finally reached that point where I was spent. I had thought I had passed that point many times already that night. Many times I was done and ready to succumb, but I always caught another wind.

The weariness was a mix of pain in every bone, connective fiber, and joint. I could no longer think, and I was losing my ability to react. My hope was gone, and I was settling into apathy. I had less than a minute worth of fight inside me but looking over the horde, we had hours of work ahead. I felt no second, third or fourth wind left inside me.

I wanted to curl in a ball and accept fate.

Bryan and Critter were tired too. Both men wielded only one sword due to exhaustion. I could see the same depletion in their eyes and the eyes of the others.

"Bryan!" I heard Tomas yell. "I can't keep this up much longer."

"Don't make me use a 'that's what she said' line," Scott yelled back. Then he said seriously, "I'm about spent too, man."

"Hold the line men!" I heard Bryan shout next to me. Then I heard him curse quieter, "Where is that damn drone?"

It was a stupid and crazy question, I thought.

My legs gave out as I stumbled on a body of the undead and Bryan caught me with his shoulder under my arm. Somehow he didn't miss a swing.

"Hold, brother," he encouraged.

"I can't," I whined. I hated myself, even my voice gave in to weakness.

Bryan let go of his sword with one arm, backhanded me and yelled, "Pull it together!"

I stood up straight and continued to swing at the unending mass. The pain and indignity suffered from the strike temporarily invigorated me.

"I see the drones! They're perfectly located." Critter declared.

I swung weakly as our line kept retreating. We, as a group, had met our match.

Adam's voice boomed through our consciousness. "Hold the line and get down when I say, 'duck!'"

I saw the vampires walk down the hill into the horde of zombies. They walked through the swarm unmolested by the undead. It appeared that those things respected the vampires as they parted a way for them to walk through. The vampires were quickly out of view. Again, I had not seen Abigail.

I could sense a palpable rise in morale in the people on either side of me. They fought with a new resolve. I could hear it in their war cries. I could hear it in the whistling, crashing blades. This seeped into me. I felt empowered. My slashes into the screaming enemy horde before me increased in power, but I didn't know how long that would hold, maybe ten swings. I kept swinging.

Bryan yelled at me over the din of combat, "I'm stepping back. Hold my place, Eric."

I was too tired to argue. I only had two or three powerful swings of the sword still in me.

From the corner of my eye, I saw Bryan pull a handgun from a holster at his appendix and aim at a drone in the middle of the zombie mob.

"Down!" Bryan screamed and it was echoed by Adam in a louder voice. Bryan fired his handgun at the drone. I was slightly deafened by the report.

I ducked just enough below the heads of my opponents, but not too much to interfere with my fighting.

As I slashed at a zombie's neck, a sudden string of explosions rocked the cove. I felt the concussion rush over us. I stood back up and saw that the drone had exploded over the heart of the zombie horde. The center was completely leveled. The zombies on the fringes were stunned by the brutality of the blast. I had forgotten that the drones were wired with explosives to prevent their captures. It seemed that when one exploded, the others blew their charges immediately. Four more explosions echoed through the valley.

Everyone around me drew their guns, and for the next few minutes the thunder of guns deafened me in the confines of the cove. I learned that war movies did not do the sound of battle justice. The endless roar of guns normally would have shattered my nerves, but in a way the loud staccato energized me. It was the battering sound of victory as we finished up the battle.

I was about to ask why we didn't just shoot out the drone causing the explosion and then shoot the zombies from the beginning, but that was answered after the few minutes when the guns clicked on empty and there were no bullets to reload. I learned later that most people had something like ten to twenty pounds of bullets on them, and that was quickly used up. Besides that, there was no manufacturing of new bullets in the Forbidden Zone, so bullets were literally worth more than their weight in gold. Again, bullets were only used as a last resort, and we had just hit that wall.

Critter took me aside and had me shoot some zombies with his firearm. He coached me to extend my arms, look through the sites with the help of the flickering torchlight, and to squeeze the trigger. It felt as if the power of the recoil was transferred into my arms and into my heart. I felt empowered in an odd way. That earlier accidental shot was the first time I had ever shot a gun. Needless to say, it scared the crap out of me. Usually, I think the word empowered is an overused buzzword. However, that was the only word that came close to explaining what I felt each time I squeezed that trigger, saw the zombie drop, and felt the explosive power go up my arms into my chest. My very soul seemed to capture and hold that power.

After shooting a few by looking through the sites, Critter had me aim simply by pointing with one hand, foregoing the use of the sites. I actually was more accurate this way. It was like simply pointing a finger at the target.

When the last gunshot echoed through the valley, we cleaned up the rest of the undead survivors with the sword. At this point, I no longer saw it as carnage. I was so spent emotionally, I no longer saw the dead as once human. It was simply clean up work that I wanted to finish so that I could wash the nasty, smelly mess off of my body and get a good night's sleep.

"Warriors!" Adam's voice boomed. "Circle up."

I looked around and saw no upright zombies or even crawling ones in sight. I scanned the hills and noticed the vampires were gone. I felt regret at not seeing Abigail. Inside I was hoping she was impressed with my swordplay. It reminded me of a soccer game I played in sixth grade when I played my heart out to catch the attention of Jill, my first childhood crush.

Abigail was a woman who may have been trying to kill me, yet there was an odd attraction. Was it the thrill of the taboo, or had the vampires really distorted my perceptions with their... Their what? Magic? Spiritual possession? I pushed that from my mind as I was not ready to face superstition or even worse, a real magic that I could not comprehend. I would save that for tomorrow. Flesh and blood zombies were more than enough for now.

We walked over the bodies, stepping on them piled many deep. There was literally no where to walk on firm earth. There was not a patch of exposed dirt in the valley. Every step was on soft meaty flesh or the hard skulls. I finally made it back behind the final barrier. The wall of undead humanity had pushed us back almost to the tents. As I placed my feet on that soil, I had never appreciated how good standing on solid ground could feel. Adam had purposely picked a clear spot of ground for us to gather.

He congratulated us. My mind was elsewhere as he gave a short speech. I was brought back when I felt a slap on my shoulder and heard people clapping. They were congratulating me specifically.

"Good job," Adam said. "I really didn't think you would make it."

I smiled at first, but saw that he was serious. He really thought that I would have wilted and died. All of them thought that I would buy the farm that night. I couldn't really hold that against them. I had thought the same from the very beginning until the last sword slash, but I was hoping others would have had some faith in me.

Adam dismissed us but kept some people guarding the barrier for any stragglers. The rest of us went to wash up. Some noncombatants greeted us with dry warm clothes after we bathed in a clean part of the creek and washed with a liberal amount of the homemade sanitizer.

The non-combatants took all of our nasty, zombie goo soaked clothes and threw them in a large cauldron and boiled them in a chemical solution. I didn't know if all that really mattered because I had been soaked in that ickiness. If I didn't get sick from that, I was probably immune unless bitten. However the next few days I worried about being stricken. Every little ache or hints of an imagined fever worried me that I would turn into one of them.

Next, we were inspected for bites. I didn't know the protocol for dealing with a bite victim and I feared it may result in an instant bullet in the head. I didn't think that I had been bitten, but with that worry in the back of my mind, I was fearful as they looked me over. The psychosomatic effect made me feel as if I had bites everywhere. However, I was clean.

With a washed body and fresh, dry clothes, I started to head back to my tarp hooch, when Critter called me over to the communal fire. It looked as if he and Bryan were buddies again. It reminded me not to take things too personally in the future when the crap hit the fan. Tempers flared, but the brotherhood and sisterhood of the sword always returned when needed.

"Where are you going?" asked Critter.

I was confused for a moment and said, "To sleep."

"Can you actually sleep?" He asked.

I considered the question. I was exhausted but still too wired from the constant deluge of the adrenaline dump. "No," I said.

"Pull up a stone and have a seat," said the red haired female warrior. She was among a number of people whose names I still didn't know.

Tomas and Robert sat with them and suddenly I felt a sense of family that I had never felt before. Not even with my adopted parents. I had felt it on the run back after the encounter with the vampires, but not as intense once the invasion halted. This simple invitation to share a campfire was one of the most special occasions of my life.

I could see it was mutual. Bryan greeted me with a smile. "Have a seat, my brother."

I realized that I stood there unable to make a decision about anything. I sat down, and heard a drone speeding into the village. I caught it from the corner of my eye in the firelight and somewhat forgot about it. My two body camera vests and ball cap were covered with zombie goo, so I had a small handheld video camera with me. No one seemed to mind as I recorded them.

"You really kicked some ass and even saved mine," Bryan said. "Did you see him in action?" he asked the others around us. "First day wielding a sword other than a kid's plastic light saber."

"Baloney," Tomas said emphatically. "Had he not shot the gun, we wouldn't have had that problem."

"Relax," Critter said. "First off, it was my fault. It was all mine. Second, we knew about that herd for a few weeks. Anything could have been the catalyst: A lost hunter, a saboteur from the Low Boys, anything. Hell, sometimes they just move for no reason. We should have moved out from beneath Damocles' Sword a week ago."

Tomas shrugged, "Maybe." Then he laughed and it seemed as if any resentment that he held in his eyes melted away.

"You're alright in my eyes," Robert said to me.

"Thanks," I said. I suddenly felt nervous. I felt like there was something I should yet do. As the new guy, I wanted to be seen doing something. "Should I go stand guard," I asked.

"That's been taken care of," Bryan said. "Tomorrow your job is to accompany a few of us into town to scavenge some supplies. You'll get to film us and we'll all be famous."

This sarcastic remark sparked a round of laughter.

I laughed with them. "OK," I said. "Thanks."

"Don't thank us yet. You're gonna have to work," said Tomas.

"But I'm done for the night?" I asked.

"If you want," said Bryan. "Are you ready to call it a night?"

As exhausted as I was at the late hour, I realized that I still had too much adrenaline in my system. I could feel it almost tingling away as I trembled from its after burn.

"I guess not, but I could sure use a beer," I said.

"Wish no further," Scott yelled behind me. "I done brang us some whiskey I kept hid."

Bryan pinched the bridge of his nose as if suddenly suffering an intense headache.

"What's with you?" Scott asked. "Is it that Adam doesn't want us having a nightcap, tonight?"

"No, no, the whiskey is fine," Bryan said. "It's just after seeing such intense slaughter and carnage, could you please not savagely butcher my English language."

Critter grabbed the bottle and took a drink. There was enough for each of us to get a few swigs.

"What's the problem then?" asked Scott.

"First off, 'brang' is not a word."

Critter passed the whiskey to me. I took a drink and caught the sound of the drone flying over the fire to get another angle. Something about it was bothering me. It wasn't fear that it would go off. It was just that I intuitively didn't trust it. I was becoming like my hosts, but it was something beyond that. I felt that it was personally spying on me.

Critter looked at me with a big grin and said to Scott, "Yeah. You should have said brung, not brang."

"OK," Scott said agreeably. "I can do that."

"No, no, no. You can't say that either," Bryan stated irritably.

"When can I use those words? Do they gotta be conjoined with some adverb or something tricky," Scott asked.

"You can't use them. Brung and brang are not words," Bryan insisted.

"Yes they is," Scott shot right back, winking at me.

Critter laughed hysterically. The others joined in. It was such a silly conversation after such an intense day, and knowing that the mortal danger was resolved, we couldn't seem to hold back our laughter and we couldn't help but enjoy the life that was gifted to us.

"No, they are not words." Bryan looked at me and said, "This is getting cut out of your documentary. They'll think we're a bunch of uneducated hillbillies up here."

"Then what am I supposed to say," demanded Scott.

"Brought. 'I brought some whiskey,' is the correct way to say that," Bryan instructed with some exasperation.

That's not right. A brought is a hotdog," Scott insisted.

"What?" yelled Bryan.

Adam yelled from teepee, "You young people keep it quiet."

We all laughed quietly.

"Yeah brat, a bratwurst," Scott said a little quieter. I couldn't tell if he was serious or just putting Bryan on. Then Scott winked at me again.

Before Bryan could go off on Scott, I said, "Scott. Scott. You cannot say I brung or brang something."

"Thank you," said Bryan.

I finished what I was going to say, "You have to use a conjunctive adverb such as 'done' before brang and brung. Such as 'I done brung' or 'I done brang.'"

"See. He's an educated journalist. That's what I done said, 'I done brang some whiskey,' with a lot of conjugating. You done need to learn English," Scott scolded Bryan.

Bryan pinched the bridge of his nose again, but suddenly burst out laughing. We all did.

I quit laughing as I watched Tomas raise the bottle in a toast, "To my brothers and sisters here tonight, who I salute. Your spirits will live forever with me."

The others voiced their affirmations.

I heard the whine of the drone backing away. As a documentarian, it reminded me of a pan out when cutting a scene. I glared at it as it slowly faded away into the night with its lens pointed at me.

Epilogue

I found out later that at that same time in an office in Virginia about a hundred miles north of the Forbidden Zone, Tommy and two government techs stood around a computer laughing. There was excitement in the air as they passed around stemmed glasses that were quickly filled with bubbling champagne.

On the computer they could see us sitting around the communal fire. They had just heard Scott defend his use of "brang," and my defense of him.

"Awesome!" yelled Tommy as he toasted his techies. "I think we have enough for a thirty minute episode and not just random scenes, but a damn good plot with interesting personalities, as well as interpersonal drama."

They watched the footage zoom back as I glared at them through the drone's camera.

"Absolutely. We just have to edit it to have the plot that we want," said one of the techies.

A loud knock pounded on the door.

"Come in, Don," Tommy yelled.

The door opened and Don's hulking bulk entered. "I just got back off the helicopter."

"I know," said Tommy.

"How is it?" asked Don.

"Very good. Eric's equipment is working great. It was worth the investment. It's not shaky at all. By the way, you were excellent out there, Don. Watch this," Tommy said as he fiddled with the computer's keyboard. "Dammit, Mr. Tempe, can you get Eric's feed."

The head techie, Mr. Tempe's, fingers flowed over the keyboard like he was the Frederic Chopin of the tech world. The screen was filled with feed from my video camera showing the men enjoying each other's camaraderie after surviving hell.

Don laughed, "As stupid as Eric is, don't you think he'll ever figure it out? That we can see and hear everything from both his cameras and the drones?"

Tommy shook his head no and said, "You have firsthand knowledge about him in action, what do you think?" It was a serious question.

Don considered it, "Right now he is only thinking of survival and fitting in. However, he's surprisingly resilient. I saw a new look in his eyes. A warrior's look."

Tommy scoffed. "He accidentally shot a gun and couldn't even stick to renouncing alcohol. He is drinking with those hillbillies right now."

Don scoffed right back, "Every single one of you would have died today, many times over." Don looked pointedly at each person in the room until they looked away. He finished by simply saying, "He lived."

No one returned Don's eye contact.

Don continued, "When he figures out how to survive and can focus clearly on his situation, he could be a force that we'll have to deal with. We need to get him with the Low Boys immediately."

"You couldn't stand him, now you sound like you respect him," Tommy said in an almost accusing tone.

Don blew out a breath and said, "He's still learning, but trust me, I'll still slap his ass around tomorrow."

Tommy agreed, "Tomorrow will be decisive indeed."

TO BE CONTINUED.

Excerpt: Book 2

Douglas Bircher swept through the dark woods on his run to escape from the Caverns of the Vampires. The black shadows of the hooded vamps flitted all around him in the chase.

His blood pounded in his ears like war drums of a pursuing tribe. His chest felt like it would implode as he couldn't take in any more air to fill his need for oxygen, but he would rather die of exhaustion than to face those things again. He had no idea how long he had run from that terrible cave of crystal, but at this point, it was purely base instinct that propelled him, driven by the howling bloodlust of those things.

Collapsing of exhaustion probably wasn't too far away. He would stumble as fast as he could about twenty-five to fifty yards on clumsy, numbed feet that barely obeyed his brain and sprawled on his face from a root, or rock in his path. Obstacles were almost impossible to avoid in the nighttime woods anyway, but in his present state the trip hazards seemed to seek him out. Sometimes an obstacle wasn't needed. It was pure fatigue that sprawled him on several occasions.

He not only wanted to save himself, he had to warn others back in his village. It was his duty as a soldier. With those two desires, he pressed on.

During his run in the sheer panic through the dark forest, he had quickly lost contact with the other two surviving soldiers. Another of their group had been consumed by the vampires. After exiting through the quartz doorway, they blindly plunged downhill. The soldiers couldn't see each other and could barely see the many tree branches with which they often collided.

Once his initial panic calmed and he realized he lost his comrades, he had rested on his belly in the leaves after he had fallen over a root, but almost immediately he had heard the screams of one of his fellows and howls of triumph of those vampire things crazed by their bloody capture. It was a scream he never expected a hardened soldier to ever make. It started out as a high pitched shrill of terror and lowered to a groan so deep as to emit from the most profound pit of hell as the man was drained and devoured. The terror voiced in that man's final moments had driven Douglas onward. He would rather run to death, only hearing the crunch of the leaves beneath his boots than hear the screams of a comrade murdered again.

On one of his final sprawls, he lay in a panting heap, thinking it was finally safe to rest, or maybe it wasn't safe but his body just refused to move. However he forced himself to hold his labored breath so he could hear the surrounding forest.

What he heard sent him into a headlong panicked run again. The sound of a predator's feet crunching leaves whispered above his thundering pulse and heavy gasping breaths.

The footfalls were slightly muffled like that of a great cat that could stalk at a full run.

He felt a sense of hope as a red line was breaking on the mountainous eastern horizon. He wasn't sure if it was truth or lore about vampires' lives being confined to the night, but he had faith that the light of the sun would be his savior. It was a bit of a metaphor from his days in Sunday school as a kid. He kept up his mad sprint, and then after a time, he slowed to a light sustainable jog.

However, he kept catching the glimpse of a blackened shape, a figure of a person in the vampiric black hooded cloak, who either trailed him, or came up on the side of Douglas as if corralling him in a certain direction. Whoever it was kept their distance, just enough to keep him moving but not close enough to catch him. He felt like a great tiger was playing with him, savoring a playful hunt before the meal.

He pushed on and caught his foot on a root, twisted his ankle and sprawled one last time. He looked up in terror as he lay at the feet of a black cloaked, hooded thing. The figure in black raised a finger to its face where its lips would be. He could not see the face, only the blackened maw of the hood, but he could see it was the universal signal for silence. He still thought it best to scream, but he found himself compelled to obey.

The figure moved its hood back as it squatted and leaned into him, readying its mouth to eat. Douglas was about to scream, but he saw the face.

It was the vampiress who had warned him to run. The one who broke the spell and allowed the escape. He wondered if she was just a sadist who prefered a chase before killing. Maybe she wanted his blood only for herself. Afterall, she had chased him far from the other monsters. He could still see the hunger for blood in her eyes, but he could see something else that may have been compassion. He wasn't sure which drive was in command of her at this moment.

"I think you are safe," she said in a soothing voice. The smile on her red lips almost hypnotized him. Aloud, her voice had the same sound as the psychic voice in his head. "Catch your breath. You are under my protection, but be cautious because I am under no one's protection," she finished with a hint of irony in her mysterious smile.

He sat up, but cowered slightly as he sized her up. She had an M-16 strapped on her back and an ornate sword at the scabbard on her hip, but no weapon in her hand. She was well aware of his distrust, but she seemed to have the confidence that she could handle him without the weapons if he tried something. That terrified him more than if she was locked and loaded for a war against him.

She said, "Morning is dawning and that is your time, not ours, but you must not go back to your village. The Specter controls those who lead it, as you already know and they will kill you, but before they kill you, they will get you to rat me out."

Douglas started to protest, "you saved me. I would never betray you."

"They have ways that you can't imagine. You must understand my predicament. It would be better for me and make my life much easier if I simply killed you."

He recoiled slightly.

"Don't worry, I have fed already. You are safe from my desires, for now."

A rustle of leaves caught Douglas' attention. A squirrel bounded by and jumped and clung to a tree trunk as she cast it a glance. Douglas saw it freeze as he and his three fellow soldiers had been frozen by a psychic command. It hung rigidly, its claws biting deep into the bark of a great white oak tree at her shoulder's height.

Douglas protested, "I need to go back to my town and warn—"

"No," Abigail growled fiercely. She drew her sword and Douglas found himself frozen in place and at her mercy again. She slashed her sword and it swung at his neck. He cringed, but it passed him by and decapitated the squirrel still clinging from the tree.

She picked up the body and turned away from him as she sucked the blood from the neck and then tossed the bloodless squirrel to him.

She squatted at eye level as she told him, "Eat this later. You'll need food, but cook this well before eating. You will be safe from catching anything I have."

"I could become a vampire if I ate it raw?" he asked. The mad craving for immortality suddenly sparked in his eyes.

She saw the burning and slapped him hard across the face. She replied sharply with disgust at his desire, "Do not confuse arrogance for immortality. Besides, most people who are infected by vampires do not turn, but rather die of insanity."

"Why are you helping me?" he asked, rubbing his reddened cheek.

She gave him a handgun with a few loaded magazines. Going weaponless in the Forbidden Zone was almost a death sentence. "I am not a monster," she replied and then instructed him, "If you need to shoot a vampire, aim for the heart or head, preferably one shot to each target. We're very resilient, just do not try to shoot me."

"You got it and thanks. Hey--" he started to say.

She stood up from her squatting crouch and said, "I must go help a friend."

"What's your name?" he asked.

She squinted, irritated by the sunlight, put up her hood, and donned very dark sunglasses as the sun was now just peeking over the ridgeline behind her.

"Who are you?" he persisted.

She turned and walked away replying over her shoulder, "Abigail."

About the Author

R.J. Burle's interests are as far flung as hunting with homemade archery equipment to spending a few years as a volunteer firefighter, from trapping and SCUBA diving and even earning a doctorate in Chiropractic. He is a student and teacher of martial arts--studying many forms throughout his life. He studied screenwriting writing at UCLA, and he incorporates that fast paced writing into his novels. The former Marine is married with four kids and credits living a colorful life with having a deeper well from which to draw inspiration. Visit him online at rjburle.com.

CPSIA information can be obtained
at www.ICGtesting.com
Printed in the USA
LVHW041346231120
672449LV00003B/268

9 781087 918587